CHANGING TUNES

By Heather Gunter

Cover designed by Robin Harper, Wicked by Designs

https://www.facebook.com/WickedByDesignRobinHarper

Interior Formatting by Tami Norman, Integrity Formatting

https://www.facebook.com/IntegrityFormatting

Edited by Raelene Green of word·play by 77peaches, a division of 77peaches enterprises, LLC

www.77peaches.com

To Tami Norman my forever friend/ critique partner/ blog partner & cheerleader.

You are the person that has been there for me from the beginning. Your support is endless and your friendship never wavering. When I was down, you lifted me up. When I said I couldn't, you said, "Yes, you can." You are the one that pushes me and keeps me on my toes. You are my person.

The beautiful journey of today can only begin when we learn to let go of yesterday.

~ DR. STEVE MARABOLI

Chapter 1

Never let them see you look weak

Suitcase in hand, my head held high and a deep breath, I slam the trunk down on my very new and very expensive car; a gift from my father. I remember the moment he gave me the keys. In his very matter of fact voice he said, "Here's the keys to your new Lexus, don't wreck it; I will be unable to accompany you to college. I have a meeting I can't miss, but I trust you will be just fine." Not a question but a statement; something I'm used to.

Glancing around, I see parents everywhere, hauling luggage. Most are grasping onto their son or daughter with all of their might and tears in their eyes as they drop their babies off at college. I notice several students looking horrified at the display of affection, but others actually seem sad to see their parents go. That feeling is alien to me. I couldn't wait to get away and start anew. Thinking of new makes me think of Miranda, my partner in crime; or used to be. For a brief moment, I think of calling her and seeing if she is faring any better than me. But the thought quickly fades as I realize I honestly don't have anything to say to her, and how awkward it would be; I don't do awkward.

Coming back to reality, I walk with a confidence I don't quite feel, but show anyway because that's the 'Davis way'. "Never let them see you look weak," as my father would say. I straighten my head, shove my designer sunglasses back up my nose, and fling my long blonde hair over my shoulder with my hand. I throw on my confident face and move towards my living quarters for the next year. I feel looks from people as I walk by—and by people, I mean guys. Some guys are flying solo, some have girls with them, and some are in a group with other guys. It doesn't matter; I certainly don't discriminate. I throw a smile or two, as I walk by and continue my strut. I'm certain I dressed perfectly for my first impression. Clad in short cutoffs that show my long, lean and tan legs and a pair of wedge sandals to make my legs look like they go on for miles. I'd thrown on a very tight white tank top that shows the perfect amount of cleavage. I am well aware of what I look like, and I use it to my every advantage. Hell, I've got it; why not flaunt it?

As I walk into the apartment building, I shove my sunglasses onto my head, let my eyes adjust to the light and pull out the letter stating what hallway and room I am in. I'd requested an apartment to myself, but apparently those are only for upper classmen. I don't know anything about whom I will be rooming with, just that my father paid for the apartment for the entire year. I continue my trek down a hallway, nearing where my room is supposed to be, when I hear a whistle. I stop, turning to where the sound originated from and spot a very nice looking guy, smiling as he leans against a doorframe, showing no shame in having been caught. He walks over and holds his hand out to me.

"Hi, I'm Austin." He introduces himself with a southern drawl. He's tall, blond, tanned, and toned from the looks of his arms.

Oooohhh, now he could be fun.

I flash my signature smile at him. "Ashley." I grasp his outstretched hand with mine and he instantly brings it up to his lips and kisses it, still maintaining a smug smile.

Releasing my hand he says, "Well, Ashley, if you need anything—anything at all—don't hesitate to seek me out. I live right here," he points to the door behind him.

All of a sudden I hear a loud female shriek, "Austin!"

"Uh oh, busted," I hear Austin grumble and watch a guilty look creep up on his face.

I turn around and see a pretty, but pissed off, brunette stampeding her way over to us. She stops, looks me directly in the eye and says, "He's taken, so get your paws off of him!"

Okay, I can fully admit, in the past, it wouldn't have mattered to me whether a guy was taken or not, but this time it's all on him. I can't be blamed for this. I'm a couple of inches taller than her and looking down, matching her look for look, I spout off, "You may want to keep *your* man on a tight leash, then, since he hit on me, not the other way around!" I turn around to make my way to my room and see a small crowd has formed from the banshee shrieking her head off.

Great.

Way to ace my first impression at college. This is what I need to avoid. Reminder to self; just don't talk to anyone. It will be so much easier that way.

I peek at Austin, to see how he's faring, and notice his tanned face quickly turning bright red. Who knew someone so tanned could show such embarrassment? He begins to pull her away and I hear him say, "Baby, I was just being friendly."

I shake my head. I can't help the smirk that pops up and continue down the hall, looking for 220C. Several guys and girls are watching the scene with rapt interest, and I can still hear Austin mumbling apologies to his girlfriend. I feel the eyes of the others watching me as I pass, but I don't pay them any mind. I walk with purpose, showing no interest in the scene behind me—as if it never happened.

I stop at a door with a small chalkboard hanging beside it. On the chalkboard is written *Mac and Ashley's Room*. It's swirly and very girly, with a couple of smiley faces around it and a heart. Who the hell am I rooming with? Mary fucking Poppins?

I just set my suitcase down to pull out my key when the door swings open, startling me, and I drop my keys. Standing in the doorway is a petite, pretty brunette, possibly of Puerto Rican heritage. I tower over her like a giant. She's smiling and puts her hand out, but quickly changes her mind and throws her arms around me. I stand as still as a statue. *This is awkward.* She pulls back and squeals, "I'm so glad to finally meet you. I wondered when you were going to get here. I've been waiting on pins and needles. We are going to be the best of friends! I can't believe it, we're in college."

"Do you ever stop talking?" I growl.

For just a moment her smile falters, but just as quickly, it's returns to full strength. "I'm sorry, I just get so excited. I guess I really should have introduced myself first. I'm Mackenzie, but everyone calls me Mac." She leans down and picks up my keys, handing them back to me.

"Thanks," I say dryly. "Ashley."

"Your stuff arrived already, and I had them move it over to the room on the left. I hope it's okay; they're the same rooms, but the window opened a little easier in the one on the right, and sometimes, I need fresh air."

Ignoring her window comment, I glance around and walk to the door of the room she indicated would be mine.

I open the door and see my boxes of things did, indeed, arrive. "It's fine."

The room is simple, a stark cream with boring brown carpet—nothing special, just a room. A room that symbolizes a couple of things I'm not willing to admit to myself quite yet.

Sensing I don't want to talk, Mac says, "Okay, well, I guess I'll let you get settled. Holler at me if you want some help."

For the first time, I acknowledge her comment and realize something myself. This is a new beginning. Some place no one knows me, or what's happened to me, or who I am.

I make eye contact with her, use her name and muster a small smile, "Thanks, Mac," hopping my eyes convey I actually mean it.

She nods her head and leaves my room, closing the door behind her.

I find the box marked bed linens, pull them out and make my bed. As soon as the bed is made, I take my shoes off and lie down. The moment my head touches the pillow, I let sleep take me.

I wake to a soft knock on the door and notice it's pitch black in my room. I manage a garbled, "Come in," and Mac enters. Light seeps into the room when the door opens.

"I'm sorry, I didn't mean to wake you, but I figured you'd be hungry and wondered if you wanted anything to eat? I went to the store while you were sleeping and stocked the refrigerator, so there's a lot to choose from. I made some dinner, if you like chicken stir-fry. You're more than welcome to some."

I'm surprised for a moment. I'm not used to anyone being so thoughtful and thinking of me. I take a moment too long analyzing and Mac quickly turns to leave saying, "Or not. I'm sorry."

"Mac, I'll be out in a minute; thank you, and yes, I like stir-fry."

She briefly turns back to me, a smile surfacing on her face, before she walks away. A feeling of calm washes over me as I realize I liked seeing her smile, and it was really nice having someone do something for me, without any expectations. I vow to be nicer to Mac, and truly use this experience as a second chance. I don't have to be close to Mac, but I can be nice to her. With that determination, I walk into the small kitchen area and smell the stir-fry that smells heavenly.

"This looks great!"

"Hopefully, it will taste better than it looks." She grabs a couple of plates and dishes out our food, setting them on the table. We sit down and begin eating in silence. It tastes incredible.

"This is really good," I pronounce, looking up at her, a pleased expression on her face as she continues to eat. Figuring a conversation would be better than eating in awkward silence I ask, "Where did you learn to cook?"

"Hands down, my dad. He's a really good cook. My poor mother can't cook worth a lick, so my dad's always been the cook in our house." I sense the fondness she has for her dad as she's speaks about him. "My dad really loves cooking, and my mom hates it, so it all works out. Do you cook?"

I snort out a, "Hell no. I've never been taught, and we had people who did that for us. Plus, my father would have a conniption fit if his daughter were cooking in a kitchen. He's got higher expectations for me." I quickly back track, realizing how that came out. "He just sees…" Instead of making an excuse, I call it like I see it. "He's a snob," I laugh out and Mac laughs with me, and I'm glad I didn't hurt her feelings. It quickly dawns on me that I care whether I hurt her feelings, or not. It's a very strange feeling, another one that I'm not used to, either.

"So," Mac drawls out. "What do you want to do tonight? How do you feel about getting out of here? I heard there's several parties going on around here at a number of the dorms and apartments." Her eyes shine bright, and she looks giddy and excited at the prospect of us going out together. And for whatever reason, I don't want to tell her no.

"Sure, why not?"

I don't have anything else going on at the moment, so what do I have to lose?

Mac jumps up, "Awesome, and I've got the perfect outfit." She runs to her room, and starts sorting through her closet.

I walk to my room and heave my suitcase on my bed, throwing it open. I rummage through, trying to decide on what I should wear tonight, when I hear Mac walk in. I turn and see her in a cute, short summer dress and a pair of high espadrilles. "Very cute." She looks pleased and begins to look at the choices I've pulled out, spotting my cowgirl boots.

"These are fantastic, Ashley. You need to wear these, but with what?" She places her finger on her lip, gently tapping it in deep concentration. I'm a little in awe she noticed my boots. I love these boots, and they go everywhere with me. I'd already decided I was wearing them. *This girl's got good taste.* Mac pipes up, "I think the shorts you have on actually will look awesome, but maybe this with it instead of the tank?" She lifts up a sheer cream floral blouse that shows off some of my back and is lower in the front. I have to wear a thin strap cami underneath it, but it will look great with my boots and dress up my shorts.

"Okay, give me a couple of minutes to dress and touch up my make-up, and we'll go."

She squeals and leaves the room, shutting the door behind her. I shake my head, wondering if I'll get used to that, and begin to get ready. I'm already doing things I wouldn't normally do. I would have never thought on my first night I'd be going out with my roommate. I didn't anticipate even liking my roommate. I had meant to be standoffish and a bit of a bitch, but I find myself unable to avoid liking her. My mind wanders as I fix my make-up. I need to find a guy tonight; someone who'll suffice, just for the night. Someone who'll make me feel good, and who's not attached to anyone else. I've been down that road before, and I'm not doing it again.

CHAPTER 2

COWGIRL BOOTS & JELL-O SHOTS

I'm not ashamed to say I'm feeling good, and pretty damn hot, as Mac and I step out of our apartment, locking the door behind us. As we near where the altercation with Austin and his girlfriend transpired, Mac leans over and whispers, "What was that scream I heard out here?"

"Oh, you heard that? Let's just say a guy down the hall has a very protective girlfriend."

Mac shrugs her shoulders and says, "Ah, you must have met Austin and his *lovely* girlfriend."

"Hey, I didn't do anything," I reply, ready to defend myself. Actually, this is the first time I haven't been in the wrong, I realize.

"Trust me, I know. I got here a couple of weeks ago, and I've already seen Austin in action. He's a horn dog. But he's a mighty fine horn dog, isn't he?" She laughs, and I can't help chuckling right along with her.

"Yes. Yes, he is. What's the story with his girlfriend? She seems very worried about his wandering eyes."

Leaning over she whispers, "I think he's always had a wandering eye, and instead of breaking up with him, she blames the girls."

"Why does she put up with it?"

"From what I understand, they've been together a long time. I think sometimes it's easier to stay with someone out of habit than it is to let them go."

Huh. I've never had that problem.

Changing the subject I ask, "Okay, where to?"

"I thought we'd start with the fraternities," she says wiggling her eyebrows.

The more I'm around Mac, the more I like her. But I tell myself to maintain the shield and to watch myself.

"Well, lead the way."

She leads us to a large house with a fraternity logo on the front. Music is cranking, and people are milling around everywhere.

This looks promising.

We walk up the walkway and into the house; it seems we make quite the impression, as two very hot guys immediately walk up to us. I see them exchange a look with each other. I'm not ignorant to this look; I've been around. The look tells me that in an instant, they've already decided which one will be paired with Mac and which one with me. I'm not naïve enough to believe we are more than just conquests to them. I know this, but in reality, that's what he is to me. He's a plaything, something to make me feel good, for just a little while. To my relief, the taller of the two walks up to me. He's surfer boy hot with hair that hangs in his eyes and introduces himself as Luke. Mac nudges me and I see the smile she's sporting. The guy in front of her must be her type. He's a little shorter than

Luke and has dark brown, short-cropped hair and a chiseled jaw. He introduces himself as Sean.

Yes, this will do for the night.

With introductions made, I grab Luke's hand and drag him away. Before we make it to the dance floor, I stop by a table loaded with every alcohol known to man and throw a couple of Jell-O shots down my throat. I plaster on a come hither smile, making him smile wider, and lead him to the dance floor. Dancing is my thing, something very few people know about me. I could dance all night long. I used to dance and thought that's where my future was headed. But then, life's a bitch, things happen, and plans change.

Determined to have a blast and feel good, I let the music guide me. It flows through my entire body and I begin to move. Luke, seems taken aback for just a moment, but quickly finds my rhythm and moves right along with me. I throw my arm back behind me and wrap it around his neck. He seems to enjoy my move; his breathing gets labored and I feel him harden behind me, as he presses into my lower back.

Not yet. Still too early.

It makes me hot that it took so little to turn him on, but I'm not done dancing. I have a goal to make him want me so bad he hurts; call me sick and twisted, I don't care. I feel powerful when they get to that point—the point of no return—and I will rock his fucking world. Not the other way around.

I continue letting the music guide my every move, and eventually feel him nibble on my ear lobe.

Nope. Still too soon.

I swing around to face him, taking away the easy access to my ears. I see frustration lurking in his eyes, but the heat is there, too. *Oh, yeah the heat is there.* I move a little bit away and fling my arms up, moving in time to the music and lift my hair off of my shoulders, seductively holding it up. Letting my hair drop, I lean in close to his ear, "Don't move. I'll be right back."

He nods his head and says, "You'd better." I wink at him, turn and strut to the table where I down two more Jell-O shots.

I spot Mac talking to Sean, still with a smile on her face. I walk over and whisper, "Don't wait up for me." I don't wait for a response and make my way back to Luke.

He looks surprised when I sidle back up against him. "You came back."

"I said I'd be right back, didn't I?" I don't wait for him to answer as I sweep in and lick his lips, pulling back a little to gauge his reaction. If he wanted me before, he sure as hell wants me even more now. A song comes on that I love, and my hips begin to sway. It draws his eyes right to them and he settles his hands on each side. I inch closer to him and close my eyes, letting the music take over and guide my movements. I'm beginning to feel pretty good. I'm still completely aware of my surroundings and in control, but I'm feeling a very good buzz.

I open my eyes and find him staring directly at me. He leans in and whispers, "God, I want you so bad."

"I know, I can tell." I say mischievously. To make sure he knows I'm completely aware of his state of want, I take my hand and rub him through his jeans. His eyes widen and he throws his head back. When his head comes back down he says, through hooded eyes, "Who are you, and where have you been all my life?"

Now. It's time.

"I'm the girl that's going to rock your world." His eyes widen at my brazen words. Leaning into him, I capture his mouth with my own, giving him a small taste of what's to come. He's a good kisser and he give's right back. I take the plunge and dip my tongue into his mouth. He's minty fresh, with a hint of vodka. I pull away, asking, "Where's your room?"

His eyes shine bright and he immediately leads me up a staircase. The moment we're at the top of the stairs, we're back to kissing as he leads us into a room, barely getting the door slammed before he's unbuttoning his shirt. I yank my shirt off and unbutton my shorts stepping out of them. I watch as his shirt comes off and take a moment to admire his physique. He yanks off his pants as I begin to pull off my boots when he stops me, "Leave them on."

I smile and yank off my cami, standing in only my bra and thong. He pauses, looking at me, and says, "God, you are so fucking hot!" I smile, strut over to him and push him roughly on the bed.

"So here's how this is going to work. You're going lay there, and I'm going to take control, and you're going to love every minute of it."

He begins to speak, "You don't want me to…" I quickly cover his mouth with mine to shut him up, hovering over him. *No. I'm in control, not you.*

I yank his boxer briefs down with his help, and pull a condom out of my boot. He quirks an eyebrow up, and I just shrug and say, "A girl has to be prepared."

I grab his swollen cock in my hands, slowly rolling the condom into place. I take a moment to stroke him gently but firmly, and a small groan escapes his lips. I stop just long enough to step out of my lacy thong, his eyes widening at the sight of me in just my boots and bra. It makes me smile and most importantly, I feel powerful.

The power turns me on more than Luke. Ready to rock his world as promised, I lower myself onto him, slowly, and he shudders in pleasure. I begin to move, up and down, setting a pace I can tell feels good for him, all the while ensuring pressure is applied in the place I need it most. Luke reaches forward to caress my breasts, but before he can make contact, I catch both his wrists and lock them firmly above his head, reinforcing my position of power and increasing my pleasure. I lean forward and trail my tongue across his lips before plunging it into his mouth again, riding him at an increasing pace. Luke murmurs, "You feel so damn good," as he strains forward, trying to lick my nipples through my lacy bra. I lean back slightly, out of his reach, maintaining control. I can tell by his labored breathing he is close, so I increase my pace, bringing myself closer to the edge. Finally giving in to the sensations, I let go. Just as I do, Luke thrusts into me firmly then stills, panting quietly. I sit for a moment, reveling in the power and satisfaction before carefully lifting myself off of him, grabbing my clothes and starting to get dressed.

Luke watches me through hooded eyes before saying "You don't have to go, you know?"

Why can't a guy just be happy they got some and let it go?

"I really have to go. My roommate is probably wondering where I am."

He laughs, "I'm sure Sean's taking really good care of her, or the other way around."

I'm not sure why, but the thought of Sean 'taking care' of Mac bothers me and I feel the need to find her. I'm no innocent, but she strikes me as different, better. I glance up at Luke and, as seriously as possible, say, "You'd better hope and pray he's not 'taking care' of her."

Pulling on my last article of clothing, I head for the door, and as I reach the knob hear, "Thanks for the ride."

I cringe at his words, but hold my head up as I open the door and quickly walk out. I fly down the stairs and begin to look for Mac. My heart starts to beat a million miles a minute. My concern for her is definitely not something I expect to feel. The place is still packed, so trying to find a short Mac is not an easy task. I bump into people, trying to get to the place where I left her. My urgency accelerates when I get to the exact spot I last saw her, and she's not there. I walk over to the alcohol table just to see if, by chance, she's there. Nope, no luck, but I finally spot Sean talking to a girl and hurry over to him.

"Where's Mac, and what did you do with her?" I ask, raising my voice.

Sean looks at me as if I've grown two heads and spits out. "She went home, and I didn't do shit to her!"

I don't care if he's pissed at my accusation. In fact, I couldn't really give a fuck less. "You let her walk home, alone, in the dark?"

"I'm not her dad. She's a big girl." The girl he's with stares daggers at me; looking pretty perturbed I interrupted their conversation.

"Well, why did she leave already, then?"

He leans into me; close enough so only I can hear, "I picked the wrong girl, apparently."

Okay, so if I was a normal girl, this statement would bother me, but I'm past the point of caring. I don't care what anyone thinks of me. Although, this is probably not a good start to building a new reputation for myself.

I let his comment roll off and, turning to the girl on his arm, say, "You've picked a winner here, so unless you're planning on putting out tonight, he's not interested."

Sean looks at me, severely pissed, and I can't help the smirk from emerging. I turn to leave and hear, "Bitch," escape his mouth.

I quickly turn back, "Oh yeah, you have no idea."

I leave him and his new conquest standing there. I don't have time for this shit, and begin to make my way out of the crowded house and finally out to the street. I quickly make the short walk back to my apartment, pull my key out and open the door. A lamp is on in the living room area, telling me she's made it home safely. I make my way to her door and tap on it gently, hoping she's still up. When she doesn't answer, I quietly open it just a fraction and look in. Mac's sound asleep in her bed. I close her door and walk into my room. I let the breath out I've been holding and start to undress.

It doesn't escape me that I'm not used to caring, or worrying about someone else. It actually floors me, and I feel like such an ass for leaving her.

Throwing on a tee shirt, I climb into bed, still feeling a slight high from the night and finally give in to sleep.

CHAPTER 3

TALES OF PIRATES AND STATELY KNIGHTS

I wake to the smell of bacon. My stomach grumbles, the smell overpowering enough to nudge my ass out of bed. I tumble out and decide to make a trip to the restroom and shower. My head is at a dull ache; just enough for me to feel it as I wonder what kind of conversation is in store for me this morning with Mac. I shower quickly, throwing my hair up in a clip, and slip back into my room to get dressed and put some mascara on. I don't like anybody seeing me without it. Call it my security blanket; although, I'm sure others consider it vanity. I finish getting ready and take tentative steps out of my room, heading into the kitchen. Mac is leaning over a frying pan and I hear the sizzle and pop of the bacon. I'm not sure how this works. This is our first morning waking up in the apartment together. Am I allowed to have some bacon, or is this her food? I feel silly for even pondering this, but I certainly can't just walk over and take some. Can I?

As if hearing my thoughts, Mac pipes up, scaring the shit out of me and I jump. Not only do I jump, but I squeak like a damn mouse, too. "Are you hungry?" She asks in her perky and happy voice, still concentrating on cooking the bacon and not turning around.

How in the hell did she know I was in here?

"Um, yeah," I say tentatively. "If that's okay?"

"Of course it is. I made plenty. You are always welcome to eat whatever I make."

"Thank you," I say, gratefully.

She doesn't acknowledge my words, instead tells me to take a seat at the table. As if sensing my hunger, she piles my plate high with bacon and eggs and sets it in front of me. "Eat," She instructs.

That's exactly what I do. Mac takes a seat beside me, and we eat in silence until I can't take the quiet anymore, especially after last night. It's a big fat elephant in the middle of the room, and it's bugging the shit out of me. I stop eating and look up at Mac, "About last night…"

Mac cuts in before I can say anything further, "What about last night? It's all good, Ash; no worries."

Okay, I totally noticed she's not upset I left her last night, but honestly, I'm more focused on the fact Mac just gave me a nickname! I've never had anyone call me Ash. You would think it's a logical option for a nickname, but nobody ever went there. What does that say about me? It feels strange, but kind of nice. I don't react to it, just let it breeze by. Mac continues the conversation, oblivious to what has just passed between us. "What classes are you taking first?"

Unfortunately, I didn't have a lot of say in my class schedule; that was all my father's doing. "I'm taking Chemistry, Applied Statistics, an English class and a

Beyond History class." I glance up and notice Mac staring at me open mouthed.

"What?" she blurts. "You must be smart or something…I'm sorry, that came out rude, but wow." She looks at me in amazement. Trust me, I am anything but amazing.

I snort, which my father would have had a fucking field day with, as I get up to rinse my plate and put it in the dishwasher. "Um no, Mac, *Daddy* wants me to be 'well rounded'," I say, sarcasm dripping from my voice and using air quotes when I say well rounded. Personally, I don't understand the logic behind his choice of classes. All I can figure is that in addition to being 'well rounded' he wants me kept busy, and—let's not forget—bored. Very, very bored. As if I would get into trouble. Briefly, my mind wonders to a time, not too long ago, when I did get into some trouble and I inwardly cringe at the memory.

Mac brings me back to the present when she asks, "So you didn't get to choose your classes? What about your major? Surely, you get to choose what you want to do for the rest of your life?"

I turn to her, pinning her with a death glare. This is a sore subject for me; one that pisses me off every time I think about it. It makes my blood boil. "No Mac, I don't *get* to choose my major. I have one all picked out for me, nicely tied with a bow. One that will ensure I follow in my father's footsteps. Unfortunately, we don't all get the luxury of choice, you know."

Mac throws her hands up in the air in surrender. "I'm sorry, I was just surprised."

I grab my purse, slide my flip-flops on, desperate for an escape. "Don't worry about it," I throw over my shoulder as I head towards the door.

I don't know where I'm going, but I can't breathe in here. I just know I need an escape from my current thoughts. I can't keep thinking about college plans, or class choices I had nothing to do with determining. I walk out the door, briefly leaning against it and closing my eyes. This has always been my life. Do what you're told and don't ask questions. A life I've never had any say in.

Taking a calming breath and getting myself back under control; I open my eyes, straighten my shoulders and take off down the hall. Up ahead I spot Austin coming out of his apartment. Remembering him being bitched out yesterday puts a little smile on my face, making me feel a tad bit better. Someone else's misery and all…

Austin spots me and his face gets a hint of pink to it.

Good to know he's embarrassed about it, if nothing else.

"Sorry about yesterday," he mumbles.

Not one to make things easy for people I say, "I'm sorry, I didn't hear you."

Sighing and looking the other way before looking back at me he says, "I'm sorry for yesterday."

Again, not making it easy for him.

"For which part, Austin? Having a girlfriend, or for your girlfriend bitching me out?"

"You aren't going to make this easy for me are you?"

"Hell no!" I say honestly, a hand on my hip.

"Both."

On impulse, I reach my hand out and he looks at it strangely, quirking his eyebrow. "Well, normally, when one puts her out hand out, you shake it, Austin." He latches onto my hand, pump it once as I say, "I will be your friend, but please don't hit on me again, especially since you have a girlfriend."

He smiles a sexy grin, which I've determined is just him. He can't help the grin, and I don't doubt this boy will always have girl drama. Dropping my hand he says, "Wow, you're kinda cool, for a girl."

"Thanks, I think…"

Austin lightly chuckles and says, "Well most girls wouldn't have forgiven so easily. They either would have pretended I didn't exist, or they wouldn't have given a damn whether I had a girlfriend or not, and jumped my bones right there on the spot."

He's honest; I'll give him that.

"I'm not most girls, Austin." I begin to turn around, but stop suddenly and swing back smirking as I say, "I'll see you around, Austin." I wink giving him my best smile and turn away, swishing my hips all the while.

I don't wait for a response; I just leave. I like getting the last word in. Am I bitch? Yeah, probably. I have no doubt I made him want me just a little more; just like I have no doubt he's watching my ass as I saunter away and out the door.

I don't have any direction in mind; I just walk. Before I know it, I've reached the campus library. I walk in, thinking it'll be a ghost town. Surely no one will be in here yet; school doesn't start until Monday. I see small clusters of people here and there; not the solitude I was hoping for. I'm still not alone enough. Doesn't that seem like a strange thing to want? I want nothing more than to be by myself, lost in my own thoughts, with nobody—especially not my father—dictating my life. I decide to scour the aisles, look for a book and find a corner to just be. Maybe indulge in some scandalously sexy book my father would totally disapprove of.

I keep watch of my surroundings as I make my way to the romance section, taking note of the different groups of people along the way. Oddly enough, it's a bit different from the groups at high school. Here, people are just together and it doesn't seem as cliquish.

I reach my destination and spot exactly what I'm looking for—something that makes me think of my mother. I gingerly run my fingers along the spine of the book I've settled on, and for a brief moment I'm taken back to when I was a little girl. I remember her beautiful face and smile. I remember sitting on my mother's lap as she read a Jude Deveraux historical romance novel. I close my eyes, trying desperately to recall every detail. I'm caught up in the desperation of remembering, and before I know it, I'm sliding down the bookcase until I'm sitting on the floor, my knees pulled up and the book clutched tightly to my chest. I remember asking my mother what the book was about, and her smiling with a twinkle in her eyes. Instead of ignoring me and telling me it wasn't a story for a little girl, she told me tales; tales of pirates, and of handsome, stately knights. She would weave her story so perfectly that I would think of nothing else, hoping to one day meet a knight that would sweep me off my feet. I can almost smell her hair, the hair that mirrors mine, and smelled faintly of strawberries. I would burrow in her arms and she would hold me tight, wrapping her arms around me.

I force myself to give up the past and open my eyes. Who am I kidding? There are no knights on white horses; they don't exist. There certainly aren't any happily ever afters; I'm a prime example of that. She left me, and I wasn't worth taking with her, obviously.

I shake my head to clear it, as if doing so will delete all the memories from my mind, scramble to my feet and begin walking. I turn the corner and bounce off of a chest—a hard one, at that.

Before I look up, I snap, "Watch where you're going, would you?"

"Me? What about you? I'm not the one with had her head down, not watching where she was going!"

I'm ready to tear this male voice a new ass hole when I finally look up, and I'm captivated by a pair of dark chocolate-brown eyes. Being the girl that I am, though, I don't let those eyes get to me.

"Are you for real? You were flying around the corner in a hurry!"

Apparently, he finds my reaction entertaining, his lips quirking up at me. It pisses me off, but I notice those lips, as well as the fantastic dark brown eyes twinkling with mischief. That's when I notice the rest of his face. He's wearing glasses one would think screamed geek, but they don't. He's got dark brown hair that's curled around his ears with a lock of it hanging down, almost to his eyes. A strong jaw most models would kill for, and he's tall; so tall, I realize I'm looking up, not straight at eye level. That rarely happens.

Shaking me from my perusal he says, "I wasn't *flying*, as you say. I was merely walking, minding my own business when this girl, who wasn't paying attention because she had her nose stuck in a romance book with some scantily dressed guy on the cover, careened into me."

My face begins to heat, and not just because he noticed the book I'm holding. I have the oddest feeling he knows I was checking him out, and strangely enough, it embarrasses me. I don't handle embarrassed well. It makes me bite back. Trust me, I've never claimed to be perfect.

"You guys are all the same. Why can't you just say you're sorry and let it be?" I spit out. I don't wait for a response. I walk as quickly as I can out of the library and head back to the one place I can go; the apartment I share with a very chatty girl named Mac. A place I now call home.

CHAPTER 4

No More Running

I quietly close the door to the apartment, and I feel horrid, like I've just been punched it the gut. I felt fine until I walked in, and now I have this overwhelming need to apologize to Mac. It's as if these living quarters make me feel guilt. Guilt is not something I'm used to feeling. I'm used to saying and doing whatever I want. I'm not used to feeling bad for my actions. I start towards my room and hear music coming out of Mac's room, so I bite the proverbial bullet and lightly knock on her door.

I hear a quiet, "Come in."

I open the door and see Mac in the corner of the room in a plush round chair. It's the first time I've been in here and I take a moment to look around. It's not what I expected. It's actually more modern and less girly than I would've thought; more sophisticated, I should say. There's a framed poster of a gymnast on the wall, which is the only thing sports related in the room. Her bedspread is done in browns and turquoise on a wood and iron bed with intricate leaves in between the slats; it's gorgeous.

"Did you need something, Ashley?"

I don't miss that she used my full name. She's not hateful, just curt. I'm not sure how to respond to this Mac.

I gingerly, and as delicately as I can, muster an apology; again, not something I'm used to doing. "I'm sorry about earlier. I know we're just getting to know one another. You don't know my circumstances, and I realize you were just asking…"

"It's okay. I hit a nerve; I get it. Just do me a favor, will you?"

Favors scare me.

Quietly I respond, "Sure…"

"It's nothing big, Ashley, so quit looking like I'm about to ask this huge, monumental favor." Again, she's not ugly, just matter of fact. "Next time you get upset with me, instead of leaving, will you please stay and talk, not run away?"

I must have this crazy look on my face. Really, this isn't a strange request; it just shocks me. No one has ever asked this of me. Honestly, I'm not used to people wanting to talk to me. It seems like such a simple request, but to me, it's not. It means something. The fact Mac is willing to talk to me, and to get to know me, is massive. It's certainly not something I'm taking lightly.

"Yeah, I think I can do that." I respond sincerely.

"Good," she says. She pats the bed across from her. "Have a seat. Now, can I ask you something without you getting upset with me?"

I slowly nod my head. "Sure."

Deep breaths, Ash, and don't freak out. Shit, I just used Mac's nickname for me.

"Why does your dad dictate what classes you're taking?"

I look away as I begin to respond. "He has expectations of me. I'm expected to be like him and he wants me 'well rounded'."

I take a chance and glance back at Mac. There is no pity on her face, only sincerity.

"Okay, change of subject."

I breathe out a sigh of relief.

I don't wait for her to pick the subject, and ask "So what did you think of that Sean guy last night?"

She wrinkles her nose up, "He was cute, but had the personality of a split pea. I'm not stupid, I knew he was only interested in one thing."

"Agreed, he was an ass. When I went looking for you, he'd already found a willing conquest. I don't think you missed anything great."

She sighs, "Yeah, I know. Truth is, I'm not ready to go there yet with just anyone."

This peaks my curiosity; I got the distinct impression last night she was ready to 'go there' with someone. "Really? Do you have a boyfriend you forgot to mention? Hey, I won't judge."

"What?" She asks surprised. "No. I wouldn't do that!"

"Then what is it?"

A sad look crosses her face, like she's been transported to another time and place. Finally she says, "There someone, but it didn't work out. It turns out my feelings were a hell of a lot stronger than his. Some people aren't who you think they are. You know what I mean?"

Her comment causes me to pause. Something about it rings true, but I quickly dismiss it.

"That sucks." I reply honestly.

As if flipping a switch, she straightens and brightens. "How about tomorrow we go out to lunch at the campus diner and scope out the joint? I need to get over this damn guy and meet someone else; someone different."

"Okay, sounds like a plan." I reply.

I begin to get up, ready to head to my room when Mac leans over and hugs me. My arms stay stiff at my sides, and I don't hug her back, but she doesn't seem to notice. I can't remember the last time I've been hugged. Hugging doesn't happen in my family, and hasn't since—I refuse to remember the last time. I pull away and get up quickly before I show a tear or worse, any sign of weakness. "Tomorrow it is, see you in the morning," I blurt out then leave, not waiting for a response.

Closing my door, I lean against it and let a single tear to fall. I wipe it away and look down at it. I haven't shed a tear in a long time, actually since that day, so long ago. Who knew it would take someone like Mac to make me feel something, to make me remember. Things from my past are being stirred up and I'm not sure why, but I hope and pray it stops.

I undress, throwing my pajamas on and climb into bed, thinking of the events of the day. Biting Mac's head off, my conversation with Austin, wandering aimlessly through campus before deciding to go to the library. Of all the books to look at, it had to be my mom's favorite author, and I chastise myself for even thinking about her. Let's not forget the rude guy rushing through the library and bumping into me, although he certainly wasn't bad on the eyes. Last but not least, the conversation with Mac and the hug that ended it. I'm still thrown and continue to think about our conversation and the fact she definitely wants a friendship with me, which floors me. I'm actually willing, and want to have a friendship with her. It doesn't escape my notice that at the end of my reflections on the day, the image lingering in my mind is of a pair of chocolate brown eyes.

Chapter 5

Endless Possibilities & Do-over's

I wake feeling better than I have all weekend. I actually have something to look forward to. I haven't felt like this in—I don't think ever. I jump in the shower, getting ready for the day ahead and all the possibilities it has to offer. Walking into the kitchen, I spot Mac sitting at the table drinking a cup of coffee. She looks up with a smile on her face, "There's coffee left."

Grateful, I smile a genuine smile that hasn't appeared on my face in I don't know how long. "Thank you." I pour myself a large cup, inhaling it, and I let the scent wash over me, upping my already good mood.

"You look happy this morning," she says casually.

I guess she's noticed my moods already.

"I guess I am." I take a chance, telling her a little more about myself. "I'm not used to having girlfriends. Who am I kidding? I'm not used to having friend's, period."

She looks a little taken aback. "You've never had any friends?"

"I had a friend named Miranda through high school, but I'm not sure we were what you'd call true friends. We hung out every day at school, and sometimes on weekends." I sigh, "She would have turned on me in a heartbeat, though."

"I'm sorry to hear that," Mac replies. "You know, we're going to change that. You and I, we are in this together, deal? A new place and a new start, none of the past to pull us down. We have each other to depend on, now. Let's look at this as our do-over."

Again, the girl has shocked me. For the first time, there's someone who doesn't see my faults and my past indiscretions. I'm starting new—a do-over. It makes me feel lighter somehow, and I know, without a doubt, this is a friendship worth pursuing and doing right.

"What if I screw it up?" I ask, worried.

A serious expression on her face, Mac says, "You won't. We'll fuss each other out from time to time, I'm sure, but we will always have each other's back. No matter what."

I nibble on my lip when I'm deep in thought. Actually, it's more like chew on it, and sometimes to the brink of blood. Now is no exception.

"Okay," I say.

She brightens, "Okay. Well, let's go check out the campus, and grab breakfast and more coffee. You never know, we may just find us a few hot guys." She says with a wink.

I love a girl that loves coffee as much as I do.

The hall outside our apartment is busy. The other students are milling around everywhere. Some look as if they've known each other for a while; others look a bit lost. Absorbing the scene, I glance over at Mac, feeling grateful. Something I've never felt, or felt inclined to feel, towards anyone. As if knowing my thoughts, she turns to me, and smiles.

Mac locks the door and we make our way the end of the hallway, passing Austin as he leans against his door, talking to another guy. We hear, "Ladies," as we walk by and can't stop the giggle that escapes both our mouths.

"That guy is never gonna learn, is he?" I ask.

"He will, one day." Unexpectedly, Mac continues, "When you're with the right person, you are willing and capable of changing—when you love someone enough. He just hasn't found the right person yet."

I glance at her and see her deep in thought.

"Well, don't tell his girlfriend, then. I don't think she'd appreciate knowing that." I say, jokingly.

Throwing her head back, she laughs, "No, I suppose she wouldn't. He already knows though. Otherwise he wouldn't be flirting like he does. He'll know though, don't worry. It will hit him like a ton of bricks. Mark my words, he will, one day, be a changed man, and it will all be because of a certain girl; *the* girl." She says with a twinkle in her eye.

I take in my surroundings when we reach the diner. It's surreal to finally be at college and among so many different people. I notice some of the male populace turn their heads in our direction, checking Mac and I out. Mac has no clue how beautiful she is; she is completely oblivious to the attention. I, of course, always have an eye out. That's how I scope out my next 'victim'. I know I really shouldn't call them that because they sure as shit enjoy it. But essentially, that's what they are. I'm always on the lookout for a hot guy I can reel in for just a short amount of time. Love em' and leave em' is my motto. I can't be hurt that way. I place my order, which will always and forever be, a caramel mocha latte.

Continuing our conversation, I tease Mac, "Aren't you the romantic."

She looks a little sheepish, "Maybe a little, but I do believe it."

"Do you really?"

We grab our drinks and Mac signals to a table. I make a point of smiling and throwing an extra sway in my step as we cross to it. We sit, sipping our hot drinks. Thoughtfully, Mac continues, "I believe there is someone out there for everyone; we all have 'our someone'."

"I'm not so sure," I say, deep in thought myself. Her belief in this perfect person for everyone kind of throws me. I think about my past experiences and can't imagine anyone ever loving me; wanting me for just me. I'm a mess. On the outside, I look perfectly put together, but on the inside, not so much. On the inside I'm scared shitless. I'm scared of the future and of what my life holds, and what's expected of me. The inside isn't pretty at all; there's really not much there for someone to love.

Interrupting my thoughts Mac begins, "Just you wait, Ash. When you least expect it, someone is going to throw you into a tailspin and you won't know what's hit you. Someone is going to see just how fantastic you are, and maybe then, you will, too." The last part she says quieter, but I hear her. Another point to Mac. She's made me like her even more. My rule about not getting attached is quickly being broken.

Chapter 6

Teacher's Pet

I get ready for the first day of classes with mixed feelings. Angst, trepidation, and excitement, all jumbled together. I choose my outfit carefully; conscious I will make an impression today. First impressions are everything. I'm not sure why I actually care; I've never cared before. I've always been the hot girl with the best of everything in my wardrobe. I always knew I looked fabulous, and did my own thing, not caring what others thought—my own drumbeat, so to speak.

I decide on a pair of skinny jeans and a flowing, sheer peasant top with a pair of kick ass espadrilles that makes me look extra tall and my legs extra sexy. I throw a little curl into my hair instead of going stick straight, just to add a bit of volume. My head is all over the place, and I stop what I'm doing and stare into the mirror. Shit! I didn't take this much time to get ready when we went to the fraternity party. This is just class, no big deal. I'm taking classes that I don't even want to take, dammit. Why is my stomach in knots?

A knock on the door stops my meandering mind, and I open it to a smiling Mac. "What time's your first class, Ash?"

Hearing her use the nickname she's given me makes me happy. I honestly don't ever want to hear her call me Ashley again. When she does, I'll know she's pissed at me.

"English class is up first at nine o'clock and then I'm free for a couple of hours. Yours?"

"Nine thirty. Want to meet for coffee afterwards?"

"Sounds good. You look excited. Aren't you nervous at all?" I ask.

"I'm a little nervous," she admits, "But more excited than anything."

"Ugh, I'm glad one of us is."

"Aw, come on, Ash, you look smokin' hot." She winks.

I begin brushing my hands down my sleeve, brushing away imaginary wrinkles.

She notices, "Wow, you are nervous."

I look at her pointedly, "I wasn't kidding. I'm not used to feeling this way. I don't know what's wrong with me."

"Picture it like high school, but bigger. There's still going to be all the different groups and the bitches. Don't forget the bitches." She laughs.

I don't laugh. I used to be one of those bitches she's referring to. Sometimes I still am, but I'm trying not to be. At least with Mac I'm trying.

Mac looks down at her watch, "Shit! You'd better hurry; you're going to be late. You've got about fifteen minutes until your class begins."

"Oh my God! I'll text you after class."

Thankfully, I packed my backpack last night. I grab it and toss it over my shoulder, hoping and praying I have everything I need. I snatch up my phone; glancing at it, I notice a new text, from my father, no less.

Warden: Don't be late. Your first class is at 9:00. Don't disappoint me.

Lovely. Way to start my morning off right.

I sigh and dash out. You know how when you're in such a hurry, you zone out? That's me. I don't even remember my rush to the building. I just know I made it to class with literally two minutes to spare.

I slow my approach, not wanting to draw any attention to myself. I can almost hear Miranda saying, "Yeah right, you love the attention, admit it."

Once upon a time, that was true. Not now. Now, I'm just trying to blend in. Trying to be better and do better.

I open the door to the room, rushing in faster than I'd intended. Heads turn my way at the flurry of activity, but I don't show any embarrassment. I have way too much practice keeping a cool look on the exterior. I glance around, looking for a seat and spot one in the middle of the room, quickly making my way over to it; aware of the appreciative looks aimed my way. I smile, making sure to make eye contact to as many of them as possible, clearly showing how confident I am. Little do they know, it's all for show.

I sit down, face forward, and finally notice the professor sitting at his desk. He's *wow*, to say the least. No, more like yummy, something definitely worth devouring. The moment our eyes meet, he winks at me. I'm taken aback. I know this can't be normal, but I dismiss it. It's not the first time I've been noticed by an older man, after all. He's tall and blond with broad shoulders. Completely different than what I was expecting for a professor. I was thinking more like bald, boring and obese. You know, like the ones you usually see in the movies. I know, stereotypes, so shoot me.

I open my backpack, pull out my notepad and pencil, and prepare myself for the most boring lecture known to man. After getting settled, I carefully, cool as a cucumber, look around a little to see what kind of 'blood' I've got in class with me. *Hhhmmm, maybe this isn't so bad after all. It's been a couple of days.* Some habits are harder to break than others, I realize, as I take in all the good-looking guys around me. Several girls are glancing straight ahead, dreamily, not paying attention to anything but the professor. I can't help but shake my head.

Snapping me from my survey of the class the professor begins to speak. "Welcome to my English class, I am Professor Forrester, and you have the pleasure of having me as your teacher for the semester." Several girls, and I do mean several, giggle at his statement and I actually feel sorry for them. Give me a break. Yeah, he's hot, no doubt. And maybe, just maybe, I may have gone there in the past, but not now. Not to say he wouldn't be a lot of fun; he sure looks like he could be.

"Here is the class syllabus. Read it and remember it well. There will be several projects in my class throughout the semester." I hear a collective groan, mostly consisting of deep voices, which makes me chuckle out loud.

Shit, didn't mean to do that.

Unfortunately, my outburst garners me some attention I sure as hell didn't want.

"Miss?" Professor Forrester raises an eyebrow at me, clearly expecting me to give him my name. I fight the urge to slink into my chair as much as possible. I refuse to slink.

"Davis, Ashley Davis" I say confidently, sitting even straighter in my seat.

I won't back down.

"Would you like to share with everyone what you find so amusing?" He's being a bit of a smartass, but there is also an obvious sparkle in his eyes as he looks at me. It's a little disarming.

"I was just thinking how excited I am about all of the projects you have for us."

"Is that so?" he responds, smiling at me.

What the fuck? Give it back to him...

I look directly into his eyes and match him, stare for stare. "Yes sir, I'm really looking forward to them."

He chuckles, *he fucking chuckles*, "Well, Miss Davis, since you seem to be so excited about this class, how about you pass out the syllabus to everyone."

"No problem," I say looking directly at him once again. I'm not giving him the satisfaction of seeing me falter. I get up and walk over to him, and I see his eyes roam over me appreciatively. I don't let him see I notice, though. I take the syllabus from him and begin to pass them out with every ounce of coolness I possess. I count how many are in each row, passing the small pile to the first person of each row. "Take one and pass it down, please," I ask nicely.

I receive nasty looks from several girls in the class.

As if I asked for this.

It seems I've also garnered a little attention from some of the male population. I pretend I don't notice. This isn't the time, or place, for flirting. I've already got enough attention directed at me.

I finish and sit back down in my seat.

"Thank you, Miss. Davis." He says with a knowing smile.

I'm dismissed, and he continues on to his first lecture of a class that now smells of trouble for me.

I try to concentrate on the class, but my mind replays, over and over, the events of the last thirty minutes. My very epic first day of class.

Shit! Not how I wanted my first day to go.

This was supposed to go easier. I wasn't supposed to make enemies with the girls now openly shooting daggers at me. I swear I can feel them. Of course, I'm no stranger to daggers.

Fortunately, I'm finally able to focus my attention and get drawn into everything Professor Forrester says. He's not boring; very animated, in fact, and seems to love the attention from the female members of the class. He'd be blind not to see it. Thankfully, time passes quickly and before I know it, class is over.

As I gather up my belongings and head to the door I hear, "Miss Davis." I stop, dead in my tracks, and turn slowly around. "I look forward to having you in my class." He smirks.

I turn back around and leave without responding. As I walk through the door, I hear, "Teacher's pet."

I don't turn or respond, I just keep walking, knowing I'm meeting Mac, and just need to get the hell out of dodge.

CHAPTER 7

THE WARDEN AND A FEW ESCAPED TEARS

I spot Mac already sitting at a table with two coffees in front of her.

Oh thank you, Lord!

"For you," she exclaims, sliding one coffee cup my way.

I give her a grateful smile, taking a sip, "Thank you."

"Are you okay, Ash? You seem a little off."

I'm normally great at hiding my emotions, but Mac seems read me like no one ever has.

"Let's just say, I made quite an impression in my first class."

"This I've got to hear," she responds with a smile.

I recap the events from class, leaving a couple of things out, like the wink and the way he looked me up and down. I'm not sure why I do. Maybe, deep down, I'm hoping it was just my imagination, or maybe it's because I'm worried Mac will think it's my fault. We are just getting to know each other, and I don't want her thinking badly of me. I would hate for her to think I did something on purpose to garner inappropriate attention from Professor Forrester. But like I said, maybe I completely misread the encounter. Stranger things have happened.

It doesn't escape me that, once again, I care what Mac thinks of me. I want her to see the new me I'm trying so hard to be.

Mac looks at me thoughtfully before saying, "You're a hard girl for any guy not to notice. They would be crazy not to. Oh, and girls can be jealous bitches at the best of times, so who cares."

I'm not sure why, but her compliment means something to me. For the first time, I'm feeling a true friendship with a girl. Someone I can talk to and be myself with. Well, the new me, anyway.

Mac tells me about her class and we chat for a few minutes. My phone buzzes and without looking, I know who it is.

Warden: Call me tonight. I want a report of how your first day of classes went. Remember, first impressions mean everything. Don't be late.

I'm dreading this phone call.

"Crap, I've got to get to chemistry." I rush.

"Yeah, I should go, too. I'll see you at home tonight." Mac says.

Home. For the first time in a long time, it feels like a home; a place I feel like going to.

"See you later." I wave my good-bye and head on over to my first class of chemistry—the class I've been dreading the most. It's not my best subject. Don't get me wrong, I do okay, but I definitely have to work at it. It doesn't come easily to me, and unlike my other classes, it only meets one day a week for half the day because of the experiments we'll be doing.

Several seats are still available when I walk in, so I'm not the last one to arrive. I grab a seat near the front. I'm going to need to be focused if I'm going to do well, expectations and everything. I roll my eyes at the thought.

Class finally starts and my teacher is a woman this time. She goes over the syllabus and her expectations of the class for the semester. She then tells us we will have a lab partner, which she'll assign at the end of the class. I'm actually glad to hear that, no pressure. I take a moment to look around, noting one of these people will be my lab partner for the entire length of the semester and wonder whom it might be.

I notice a guy a few chairs down from me that looks vaguely familiar. Considering I haven't technically met anyone other than Mac—well, and Luke I guess—I wonder why I recognize him. I turn around to take another look and see him glancing around the room.

On his face sits a pair of glasses I've definitely seen before. I stare harder, and the moment our eyes meet, I remember. The library; the book, and running into a hard chest, and those dark, chocolate-brown eyes. The same eyes I remember falling asleep thinking about. How is it I can remember his eyes so vividly from behind his dark rimmed glasses?

He doesn't acknowledge me, but it looks as though he recalls me, too. I quickly turn away before my face catches on fire from embarrassment.

Ashley Davis doesn't get embarrassed. What's my problem?

I brush it off, chastising myself for getting distracted and pay close attention to the Professor. Many, many scribbled notes later, we are instructed to stay in our seats until our lab partners are called. She explains she will be pairing us, starting from the bottom of the list alphabetically and pairing with the beginning of the alphabet. I should be paired rather quickly then.

She calls a Zuckerman and an Allen first. Next is a Yang and a Bailey. Who knew waiting to see who you will be paired and sitting with all semester could be so nerve wracking? A Whitman is called, and then my last name, Davis. I raise my hand, glancing around the room to see whom my partner is, only to see the guy with the glasses has his hand raised as well.

Oh, holy hell. What are the odds?

Once we're all paired, everyone begins to scatter and leave. I gather my things; taking my time in the hopes 'Whitman' will be gone. I don't let my eyes wander, but keep them focused on the task at hand and finally sling my bag over my shoulder.

I turn, only to bump into a hard chest, again, a slight *eeep* escaping me.

"Hey, slow down. Do you always make a habit of rushing around and bumping in to people?" It's not a sarcastic comment. No, the comment is said teasingly. Except, I'm not in the mood for teasing. This guy seems to bring out the worst in me.

"Damn, you are in my way!"

He tilts his head to the side, examining me. "Well, I thought, since we are going to be lab partners, I should introduce myself."

"Sorry," I say. I'm not completely bitchy, but not really sorry either.

He extends his hand, "I'm Zeke, and you are?"

I grab his hand to shake it, and when our hands touch, warmth spreads through me. Surprised at the sudden sensation, I quickly drop his hand, feeling the need to flee.

"Ashley," I finally manage to mutter. "Look, I really need to go. I guess I'll see you next Monday?"

He gives me a strange look, oblivious of my need to escape. "Um, okay," he says. He hands me a folded up piece of paper, which immediately shoots one of my eyebrows up.

"This is my number. Can I get yours?"

"Why do I need your number, and why do you need mine?" I ask.

"Well, since we are going to be lab partners and all…" He drawls out. "We are going to want to help each other, and if we need to ask a question, we can get in touch … over the phone…" He's beginning to sound slightly sarcastic now. Okay, ditch the slightly, extremely sarcastic.

I'm a little slow on the up take. "Oh. Sorry."

"What? Did you think I was trying to hit on you?" he asks with an annoyed laugh.

He's making fun of me now. "No, I…didn't…" I stutter out.

"Guess what, sweetheart? Some of us have scholarships we have to maintain. We aren't all here on our daddy's money."

How did he know that?

I've never been at a loss for words. Never. Without even having a conversation with me, he's nailed me.

"So I'm guessing by your reaction, you aren't used to guys not hitting on you? Well, then consider me your first."

I've also never felt the need to cry, or let anyone see me cry; especially not a guy, and yet, right now, that is exactly how I feel. I will not give him the satisfaction of seeing my tears.

"Asshole!" I blurt out and rush away as fast as I can.

I think I hear my name being called and a possible, "Wait" and "I'm sorry." But I'm so angry and upset I don't stop. I just need to get out of there and far, far away.

On my way home, my phone rings and I glance down to see *Warden* flash across the screen. I may as well get this over with.

"Hello, Dad."

I guess he didn't have the patience to wait for me to call him.

"Ashley, did you make it to your classes on time?"

He says my name so formally. There's no 'Hi, honey, how was your first day?' or 'I miss you being around the house.' Just, 'did you make it to your classes on time…'

"Yes, Dad, I did."

"Good, you know first impressions mean everything. I've got my money invested in your education, so don't mess it up by doing anything stupid."

My emotions get the best of me. My eyes begin to puddle as my voice begins to waiver. I spot a nearby bench and take a seat.

Choking down my emotion, I say, "I won't."

"Good, that's what I want to hear. Call me by the end of the week. I want a full report on your classes."

"I will."

"I have a meeting to get to. I'll talk to you at the end of the week."

With that, he hangs up.

I don't want anyone on campus to see my cry, so I pull my legs up and rest my cheek on them, looking in the opposite direction. I desperately try to reign in the emotions and the tears that want to fall. The tears I haven't let fall in such a very long time. I feel helpless, like I have absolutely no control over anything in my life.

I feel a hand on my shoulder and quickly look up, wiping my face as I do. I don't want anyone to see me upset.

"Ashley, sorry if I startled you. I called your name, but you must have not heard me."

I can't help the snarl that comes out. "What do you want?"

Zeke is standing in front of me. No matter how much of a douche bag he was, his presence still seems to elicit a feeling in me that weirds me out. Not in a bad way, unfortunately.

"Look, I feel bad for being such a dick." He sounds sincere, so I look up at him. He actually does look like he's sincere. Being the bitch I am, I let him stew for a moment before declaring a cease-fire.

Zeke sighs, "I'm really sorry, I don't know why I acted that way. I'm sorry if I upset you."

I glance away then finally look back at him. "I'm not upset because of you." I snap.

That's a lie. A partial lie, I tell myself, anyway. I snatch my bag and stand up. It isn't until I stand that I really notice Zeke's height again. I'm always so tall compared to most guys, but with Zeke, I have to look up. I like it a lot. I also notice he's broader than I first thought. Not as wide as a football player, more like a baseball player.

I back up, trying for some much needed space, completely baffled at why I'm thinking about his shoulders and his height, or why, at this moment, I'm paying attention to what he's wearing, especially his shoes. Dark denim jeans, a tight red t-shirt and charcoal grey Chuck's. I shake my head to clear it and find myself looking back up at his face. I don't know why, but his glasses are so hot. He's completely hot. Apparently, shaking my head didn't do the trick.

Move your ass, Ash, and walk away. Great! Now I've resorted to talking to myself.

I sigh and reach into my bag, pulling out a sheet of paper and my pen. "Here's my number." Slapping it in his hand, I turn and make my way home.

Zeke

College is something I've worked long and hard for. I have a plan, a plan that does *not* include a tall, leggy, gorgeous blonde. I knew it was the same girl in class—the one that ran into me at the library and mouthed off. The funny thing is she wasn't apologetic, not really, and I liked it. One might call me a sick bastard, but there was just something about her, something intriguing and something sad. She says what's on her mind, that much is obvious, and I like that about her. But at the same time, she can't hide the sadness emanating from her; her eyes show it, all too clearly.

When she ran off at the library, I had already seen her crouched down on the floor, clutching a book with all her might. It was the most beautiful and touching sight I'd seen in a long time. I could tell she was somewhere other than the library right then. My guess was she was inside a distant memory, one that obviously caused her deep pain. I know all about pain, so I know it when I see it.

I'd quietly walked away, wanting to leave her alone and not interrupt, even though seeing her like that had made me want to hold her and take away the pain. I didn't know this girl from Eve and yet, I wanted to protect her like no one before. Not entirely true, just one other.

49

When I'd turned the corner and we'd collided, I wanted to grab hold of her then, but how weird she would have thought me to be; a complete stranger. She'd have freaked out for sure. She was even more gorgeous standing tall, with her hand on my chest, bracing herself for the fall. Her full lips slightly parted, and her big blue eyes looking up at me in shock. I was surprised by her outburst, and couldn't help smiling a little at her. She was something, all right, and I thought about her for the rest of the weekend, wondering if I was going to bump into her again.

What luck when I walked in to Chemistry and saw her sitting in her seat, not paying attention to anything, or anybody around her, just looking straight ahead. There she sat, deep in thought, giving the professor her rapt attention. She stumps and intrigues me, this girl. Then, as if things couldn't get any better, I'm paired with her as my lab partner. This could be a good, or a bad thing; she could prove to be a major distraction.

If I'm being honest, asking for her number was something I needed as her lab partner, but there is definitely more to it. When she thought I was hitting on her, which I wasn't, really...I acted like a dick because her assumption pissed me off. Well, I was pissed off for a number of reasons: one, obviously this kind of thing happens to her a lot; and two, the thought of another guy hitting on her. I have no ties to this girl, other than the fact she's my lab partner, and yet, I was getting pissed off.

I certainly didn't need to pull the 'daddy' card on her. I can tell she comes from money. You can see her designer clothes from a mile away. I may be a guy, but I'm not completely stupid. I've had girlfriends that wore designer labels, so I'm familiar with the look.

I felt so bad I had to run after her. She didn't hear me call to her in the classroom, or if she did, she ignored me. I had to go after her. I didn't want her upset; especially not because of me, and the way I acted.

I could tell she'd been crying when I reached her and felt like a total fucking heel. I don't know what the hell it is about this girl that affects me so much, but man, she does. I wanted to grab her and pull her into my arms, and tell her how sorry I was, but when she said it wasn't about me, I halfway believed her. There's certainly more to her than meets the eye. I just hope whatever it is doesn't mess with my plan.

I have to keep to my plan, to stay at arms-length from everyone, and keep my nose in my books. Nobody's going to pay this guy's way. I'm on my own here, and I can't fuck up my future, especially for a tall blonde that makes me go all caveman, wanting to protect her and tell her everything is going to be okay, without even knowing who she really is.

I'm stickin' to the plan.

CHAPTER 9

DOUCHEBAGGERY

Mac texts me when I'm almost home, saying she'll be there shortly and—the best part—she's bringing dinner home. *Holy hell, how lucky am I?*

After the suckage that was my day, I'm looking forward to Mac getting home. How odd that, in just a few days, I already can't imagine her not being here with me. She accepts me and doesn't know my past. She brings a light into my darkness. I've never thought I was in the dark until this very moment. But it's true. My so-called life isn't the greatest, and I don't have much to look forward to, but Mac, she brings something into it that makes it lighter. It doesn't feel as hazy and miserable with her in it.

I walk down the hallway towards my front door, and I see Austin and a couple other guys chatting in the hallway.

What is it with hallways?

My plan is to continue walking and ignore them, but I'm spotted almost immediately. "Hey, beautiful." Austin says.

"Hello, Austin."

I still intend to walk on by, but my plan is thwarted by the guy next to him.

"Hi, I'm Nick."

I sigh and, trying to be the nice girl, smile, "Hi, Nick, nice to meet you."

"Aren't you in my English class? Professor Forrester?"

Shit fire and light a match.

If the floor could have swallowed me up, I'd let it.

"Yep."

"You sure made quite the impression on him, as well as a few others in the class, me included." He sneers with appreciation, chilling me to the bone. He doesn't hide looking me up and down, and back up again.

"I have to go." I say, trying to escape. Unfortunately, Nick doesn't get it, and isn't taking the hint.

"I think our esteemed professor has a thing for our girl Ashley." He directs to Austin. Austin isn't as dumb as I first thought because he sees my discomfort.

He looks at Nick, "Quit being a dick, dude. You know we've only heard rumors, and Ashley's too smart to get involved in that kind of shit."

Now I'm intrigued, and a bit concerned. "What are you talking about, Austin?"

He looks uncomfortable, but answers, "There've been rumors of girls throwing themselves all over Professor Forrester. Nothing has ever been proved, just rumors."

I decide to squelch these rumors immediately, especially not knowing what kind of game Nick is playing. "Look, I'm not that kind of girl. I don't date, or throw myself at, my teachers. Never have, and I never will."

Austin punches Nick in the arm. "Asshole!"

Nick hollers and rubs his arm. I throw a grateful smile to Austin, mouth a thank you, and continue on to my door. Once there, I open it, throw my crap down and launch myself onto the couch.

I rub my temples with my hand, trying desperately to ease the beginnings of a headache, as well as trying to contain the tears threatening to escape, again. This time, I allow a few to trickle their way down my face, too tired to fight them anymore.

I think of what Austin just said about Professor Forrester, and my intuition when he'd looked at me. I wasn't crazy after all. I think about Zeke and wonder why my thoughts seem to veer back to him. And, unfortunately, I think about my dad and the lack of feelings he has for me.

It isn't long before my eyes drift close, and for a change, it isn't dark chocolate-brown eyes I see, no, it's the eyes that look almost exactly like my own. I see my mother and me, and try to remember what it felt like to be held, like I was something precious and dear. My thoughts are interrupted with the door opening and closing.

"Did I wake you?"

I sit up, "No, I was just thinking of my suck-ass day." I smell the food wafting from the bag she's holding and change the subject. I don't want to think or talk about it anymore.

"Smells so good." I say, my mouth-watering.

"I thought we might need a pick me up dinner after our first day of classes."

I love how this girl thinks.

I stand up, grabbing some plates and utensils while Mac pulls the take out containers from the bag. We sit down at the table and talk the entire time, like two people that have known each other longer than the few days it's been. I laugh and it's genuine, and I've never felt more accepted. My phone buzzes and I get up to grab it hoping it isn't the Warden. To my surprise it isn't. It's a number I don't recognize until I read the message:

Hi, this is Zeke and now you have my number. Just in case you may have thrown it away because of my douchebaggery. I'm sorry again. I hope you have a good night and I'll see you on Monday.

"You're awfully quiet," Mac says. "Everything okay?"

"Yeah, it's just my new lab partner, Zeke."

"Zeke, huh?" She says teasingly. "What's he like, and more importantly, what does he look like?"

"Um, let's see. He's tall, dark and geeky-hot."

She laughs, "Geeky, huh?"

"No, he's not geeky," I laugh. "He looks smart and he wears black rimmed glasses, and he's got a nice body, as far as I can tell, anyway." I place my finger on my lip and tap gently while I think. "Oh, and he wears Chuck Taylor's."

"That's a point in my book," Mac laughs. "He sounds hot, though."

I think hard before answering, "He really is. He's got longer dark brown hair that curls around the edges; he has one hell of a tan going on. But his eyes, his eyes are like dark chocolate."

Mac looks at me and says, with all seriousness, "Even with his glasses on, you could see how dark his eyes were?

Damn girl, you must have gotten close to him to notice such detail."

I must be blushing, "I've maybe, possibly, ran into to him by accident, so I didn't have a choice but to notice."

"Do you like him, Ash? It sounds like there may be some interest there, especially if he just texted you. Me thinks it may go both ways." She winks at me.

I chuckle nervously. I can't even imagine, and I don't think I can, or will, go there. The Warden would skin me alive if I let anyone, or anything, distract me from my studies.

Shudder the thought; insert sarcasm.

I honestly don't need any distractions. Plus, I can't imagine someone of the male sex seriously wanting to spend time with me; or wanting me for me. Most just want to do things to me.

I excuse myself, and veg out in my room for a few before going to bed. I don't have class on Tuesday, so I'm going to spend it re-reading the chemistry chapters and my notes.

I've become a very unexciting person. Miranda would be completely embarrassed by me. It's sad, but the thought makes me laugh. How is it, in such a short time, Mac is a better friend than Miranda ever was? I think about my past behavior and I'm floored beyond belief.

I never want to be that person again. I never want to pull those stunts, and be the girl who would hit on another girl's guy. I refuse to be the old Ashley. I look at myself as new and improved; or at least trying to improve. I'm not her anymore. My mind briefly drifts to Professor Forrester, and what the old Ashley would have done. I wouldn't have given two shits about him being a teacher. I so would have gone there. I'm ashamed, and that's how I know I'm not that person anymore. That's how I know I'm different.

I haven't been the same since the night, several months ago; although, it feels like a lifetime ago. I shudder when I think about that night, but I'm thankful it was a better outcome for me. It could have been bad, oh so bad. Thinking about my past, and all the shame I feel, makes me break. I finally let more than just a few tears flow down my face. I realize sometimes, it's okay to let it all go.

I decide this weekend warrants another outing and a release. I need to be in control, if only for a little while.

Chapter 10

Priorities & Photographs

Zeke

I got back to my dorm room, grateful my roommate, who I know absolutely nothing about, is not there. Lucky for me, he spends all day, and most evenings, gone. I think he actually has a girlfriend he stays with most nights. It doesn't bother me, quite the contrary, in fact. It'll give me a chance to study without any interruptions.

I still feel like an ass, and on impulse, text Ashley. I can't leave it alone. *Oh, hell no.*

I realize after I text her, that in a twisted way, I wanted to apologize again. More importantly, I wanted her to know she was on my mind. I can't stop thinking about her. The sadness in her eyes haunts me.

At the same time, I know she's way out of my league, and I again question what the fuck I'm doing. I continue to remind myself it needs to stay only lab partners; school related stuff. I can't afford to mess this up. I have too many people counting on me, and I don't want to let anybody down. There's definitely too much riding on me succeeding.

I think about home and the ones that matter. No one here matters. She's just a girl with a pretty face and a good body. After all, my life's been far from perfect to this point.

I yank my wallet out of my back pocket, lie down on my bed, and pull out a crinkled photograph. I rub my thumbs around the edges and caress it. The love I feel is undeniable, and I resolve to get my priorities in check. I miss her so much, and my heart physically aches being away from her. I question myself, for the millionth time, whether I've made the right decision.

Next class, it's work and school alone. Nothing else matters except who's at home; who I left behind.

Chapter 11

Sex is just sex

Friday night couldn't get here fast enough. I'm about to come out of my skin, and I'm chomping at the bit to get out. I begin to get changed for a night out when I receive an impromptu text from my father.

Warden: Are you studying and staying out of trouble?

Weenie (Yes, that's me): Yes, sir.

Warden: I expect the best out of you, and expect you to not embarrass me. There are people watching you that will report back to me. Don't disappoint me, Ashley.

Weenie: I wouldn't dream of that, sir.

In my head, it's sarcastic, but fortunately, in a text, he won't know the tone accompanying my response.

Warden: See that you don't.

That was it, end of story. Nothing warm and fuzzy, but they have never been expected, anyway. Isn't that a nice way to start my Friday night? I decide to not let this 'conversation' with my father bother me, or screw with my night. I've studied and have done everything a good little girl is supposed to. I need to let loose and be free. I know exactly what I need, and walk over to the closet and begin rummaging through it when I hear a knock on the door before it opens with Mac saying, "It's me."

I giggle. Yeah, I, Ashley Davis, freaking giggled.

"I know, goofy, who else would it be?"

"Oh I don't know. Maybe a tall, dark handsome guy who wears Chuck Taylor tennis shoes?"

"Ha, ha, Mac."

I skim through my selections and decide on a sheer blouse over a spaghetti-strap tank with my skinny jeans and some flats this time. At least I won't appear Amazonian, compared to the majority of the guys around here. If I'm lucky, I won't be wearing them long, anyway. Apparently, my lack of heels doesn't go unnoticed.

"What? No heels today? No espadrilles, or boots? I'm shocked at you, Ash!"

"Nope, not tonight. I'm so tired of being so tall compared to a lot of guys."

"Well, I, for one, would love to be taller. I would almost kill to be taller," she says teasingly.

I chuckle, "Trust me, Mac, it's not all it's cracked up to be."

Mac grabs my hand and pulls me in front of my mirror. "Look at you. Do you know how many guys turn around when you walk by?"

I smile sheepishly, "Maybe."

Mac throws her head back and laughs, "Of course you do."

I resume getting ready and decide to tell her my intentions for the night. I'm taking a huge risk, but I would rather be honest. Hopefully, she won't think less of me.

"So…" I begin and avert my eyes, too ashamed to meet her gaze. "Tonight, I plan on finding someone to fool around with." I finally take the chance and look at her. There's no shame on her face; it's completely neutral. I feel like I can breathe again.

"No problem, Ash, I'm a big girl. I can tell you're itching to get out. It's cool, so no worries, okay?"

I don't know how I got so lucky with Mac as a roommate and friend, but I thank God I did. It could have turned out so differently, and I shudder at the thought. This is a huge step for me, telling people my feelings, but with Mac, it seems so much easier than it ever has been before.

"Hey, Mac?"

"Yeah," she says turning to me.

"I just wanted to tell you how glad I am you turned out to be my roommate and not someone else."

We stand there for a few seconds not saying anything. She seems surprised at my declaration. I fiddle with my fingers, intertwining them in and out in a nervous motion.

She smiles a genuine, happy smile. "Me too, Ash. It's about time you figured that out. I am made of complete awesome."

I shake my head and laugh, "Yeah, you are." I change to a serious tone, I truly am grateful she is who she is, and she's accepted me so easily. "Really, thank you for being patient with me."

"Ash, I wish you saw how wonderful you are. One day you will see it; I swear it. I got pretty lucky, too, you know…Okay, I'm heading out to finish getting ready. Do you want to hit the party at the other end of campus, or did you want to go to the club?"

"Let's do the party first, and if it's a dud, we'll venture to the club."

"I think Austin said he was going, a lot of people from the building and from my classes are going, too. It's supposed to be a happening thing." Mac grins slyly, "You never know who we may run into."

I ignore the innuendo, knowing full well whom she's talking about, and continue getting ready. I slide into the bathroom and decide to put some curls in my hair, instead of ironing it straight like I normally do. I'm feeling rebellious and the need to do something crazy.

Down girl. I certainly can't afford to get into trouble. The conversation with my father replays in my head. Yes, no trouble. I just need a release—a release from a really hot guy.

I shake my head to clear it of all of these thoughts and stop at Mac's room, seeing her grab her purse. "Ready to go?" I ask.

Mac looks up and says, "Ooohh, Ash, nice hair. Heels or not, you are going to have those boys on their knees. Just you wait."

I smile, "You are way too much, Mac, let's jet. I'll drive."

I don't think I've ever smiled as much as I have this past week.

Once in the car and headed to our destination, I'm compelled to make sure she's one hundred percent sure she's okay with me doing my thing.

"Mac, are you sure you're fine with me leaving with someone?" I rush on… "I'll leave the car keys with you, and I can always take a cab."

"I will be fine," she says. "Quit worrying. I know people that will be there. Some of them are actually very responsible, and don't drink at all, so getting home won't be an issue."

I turn to her for a quick second. "Are you sure?"

"I wouldn't say it if I wasn't. Quit worrying. You've had enough to worry about this week. This is about dancing, meeting new people and having fun, and you being able to let loose without an impromptu text from your father."

I'm silent for a couple seconds as I park the car, thinking. Finally, I ask, "How did you know?"

"Believe it or not, I can already read your moods. You get sullen, and I heard your phone buzz. I know when you're upset. Your moods always change after your phone buzzes. You did it earlier this week. We were in the living room, and I saw you look at your phone after it buzzed then put it down. You weren't the same afterwards." She taps her temple and says, "I'm smart like that."

I'm not sure what to say, so I stay quiet.

"If you don't mind me asking, and you certainly don't have to tell me, but what does he say that upsets you so much?

It's strange, but I trust her already, and feel comfortable enough to tell her. I take a deep breath before responding, "He tells me not to screw up."

I see her eyes bulge and her mouth drops open. "Are you serious?"

"Serious as a heart attack," I respond back.

"Wow! It's all I've got. I mean, Ash, you've done nothing, but do what you're supposed to this week. You've not done anything but study your ass off when you weren't at class. It's all you've done."

"Yeah, I know." I sigh.

I concentrate on the road and let my thoughts drift for just a moment. And herein lies the problem. I have no control over my own life. I feel stifled, like I'm being smothered, and I'm always on his bad side. I can't do anything right. Yep, that's me, Ashley Davis; the perpetual screw up.

Mac begins talking and I tune back in to her.

"Tonight is your night for some fun. Let's dance and dance, until our feet ache."

We make our way to the party, which seems to be really happening. The music is pulsating so loudly, the walls seem to be shaking. It's very club like, and I love it! We walk in, and I'm on cloud nine. This is heaven for me. I let the beat of the music wash over me, and Mac, sensing what I need, grabs my hand and leads me to the make shift dance floor. We pass a slew of guys, but I'm oblivious. I just need the music. I need it to lead my body and take me away from everything. An Ellie Goulding song called *Burn* comes on, and I'm gone. I love songs with heart that give my dance moves meaning. I sway, back and forth, and lose myself in the beat. Mac's right there with me, feeling it, and dancing like she needs this just as much as I do. I close my eyes and stay in my little bubble.

Several songs go by and we dance and dance. I'm sweating like a pig and I don't care. Not one bit. All of a sudden, I feel a warm body sidle up behind me and I see Mac's eyes go up. She mouths, "Hot!" She obviously gives her approval, so I don't stop. I just dance, but I see Mac make her way over to a group she seems to know.

Without turning around, I can tell he's got a nice, rock hard body, full of muscle. He's slammed up against my back and rubbing his arms up and down my arms, making sure I feel every part of his anatomy. He eventually takes his hand and moves my hair to the side and begins kissing my neck. It feels so good, but I won't let him take control, that would defeat the purpose, so I turn around. He's very nice looking, with short-cropped dark hair and a tad taller than me. Of course I'm not wearing heels, but with heels he'd still be just a tad taller. I don't know why I'm so hung up on his damn height. Of course, there is someone a hell of a lot taller, and my mind fills with images of dark chocolate-brown eyes, and the tall completely off limits lab partner they belong to. I mentally shake the image away, focusing on the here and now. I smile my come hither smile and he's a goner. I can tell by the look on his face I have him—hook, line, and sinker. I can also tell by the look on his face he thinks he's conquered me.

No way, big guy, not by a long shot. Little do you know, it's the other way around.

I wrap my arms around his neck and decide to pull a fast one on him. I can't let him think he's the one with the pull. I lean in close and use my arms around his neck to pull him closer to my mouth. He comes willingly, but I see the initial surprise light up on his face. I tease his lips, outlining them with my tongue. When he begins to moan, I slide my tongue into his mouth, giving him just a taste of what's to come.

He leans back, out of breath, looking me in the eyes, and whispers, "Who are you?"

I smile, knowing I have him exactly where I want him, and it feels so good.

"Want to get out of here?" he asks.

"Not yet, but soon. I still want to dance. I don't look this good for nothing, and I may as well make the most of it," I wink.

He chuckles, taking a moment to eye me from head to toe and back up. "And you do look gorgeous. Just as long as you dance with me, and only me."

"Hmm territorial, are we?" I tease.

"Yes, when it's something I want, you bet your pretty ass I am. What's your name?"

"I didn't know we were doing names," I joke. "I'm Ashley."

"Well, Ashley, I'm Joe, and I live in this here establishment." He takes his arm and swings it out gesturing to our surroundings.

He's kind of funny, and cute as hell. Maybe he could be more than a one-time thing? I guess it all depends on how the 'after' goes.

"It's hot in here and we've been dancing for a while. Do you want to get a drink?"

I nod and we set out to the table full of liquor bottles. A beer keg sits at its left. Several shot glasses are upside down on the table. I grab one, righting it and grab a bottle of Vodka, pouring myself a shot. I down it and go for round two. That should last me, and it'll be enough to dull my senses just a tad.

"Wow," he says, amazed.

"What?"

"I think you were made for me."

"Why, because I can handle my liquor?"

"You downed it like a pro."

Shit, the last thing I want to do is talk about my drinking habits with this guy. I just want to get my release, have a little fun, and dance; yes, dance.

I begin to feel the effects of the second shot. "Let's dance, I say grabbing his hand and leading him back onto the dance floor. A new song by Eminem comes on, and I'm, once again, lost in it. This is not a grinding song, this is a dance by yourself kind of dance song. I decide to have some fun, and see what he's made of. Let's see if he can keep up.

I glide in place doing my thing and see him smiling, liking what he's seeing. He moves with me, keeping up, but doing his own thing. So it seems the boy can dance. All right. He took my challenge and passed with flying colors. The song changes to a sexy, grinding song and I see his face light up in anticipation. As we get slammed back together he says, "You're fun. How have I not met you yet?"

"I've been around."

"What classes are you taking?"

I don't want to talk. I don't want to build a relationship with him. He's a nice guy, and I don't want to be a bitch, but I don't want him to know any more about me than he already does.

Deciding it can't hurt to tell him, I keep it vague, just telling him the basic names of the classes. Thankfully, he doesn't ask for any more information.

Instead he says, "Wow, beautiful and smart, a lethal combination." His eyes twinkle and it seems he's being genuine.

Must be careful with this one.

I don't respond to his comment. Definitely not a good idea; I don't want to give him any false hope. I glance around to check on Mac and see her in the same place as before. In a group of people, with a guy standing right next to her listening and holding onto every word she says. He looks smitten with her and I smile at the thought. She deserves to be happy with someone.

Joe interrupts my thoughts, "Hey, who are you looking for? A boyfriend to walk through the door, perhaps?"

I laugh, "Um no, no boyfriend. Just making sure my friend is okay."

I don't wait for him to reply; quite frankly, he's talking way too much. I'm not planning on courting him, for shit's sake. So I do what I do best, I use my assets to gain his attention and put his mind elsewhere, on me, and some hot sex.

A song comes on that screams me, *American Girl* by Bonnie McKee. *The Warden would be so proud.* I let the music take me to a place I haven't been since the previous weekend, and it's been far too long. I need this, this stress relief. I want to get him so hot and bothered that he lets me do all the work, which is what I need. I swing my hair and my hips, making sure to get as close to him as possible, grinding myself into his leg. I see his eyes darken and know I'm getting him exactly where I want him. While hanging onto his arms I lean myself back just a little bit, getting my hips as close to him as possible. I lean back up, and whisper in his ear, "You ready to get out of here now?"

He doesn't answer with words; instead, he just takes my hand and pulls me away from the crowd. I catch Mac's eye so she's knows I'm leaving. She winks at me, smiling, signaling for me to enjoy myself. I can almost hear her saying it. I follow Joe down a hall, and he finally stops at a door, swinging it open. The moment the door's shut, he says, "It's about fucking time."

I shove him towards the couch and straddle him. He begins to do the things I deem as a big no-no. He tries to kiss my neck, grab my tits, and I just can't let that happen. This is about me, not him.

I pull his hands from my breast and hold them up. "This is how it's going to go. I'm in charge, and you do what I say, got it?"

Being in charge makes me hot, and I can tell by the look on Joe's face, he's certainly not going to complain.

"Okay," he says breathlessly. "Whatever you want."

Joe really knows how to kiss, and he's hot, which helps. Too bad this is going to be a one-time thing. He's the kind to get attached, and that, I just can't do. I release his arms and allow him to put them on my waist. I kiss him senseless, and drag myself across his cock, rubbing and getting him so worked up, all he wants to do is screw. He tries to pull my shirt up and over my head.

"Nuh uh," I say to him, shaking my finger at him. "I'm in charge, remember?"

He grunts in response. I slowly, teasingly my slide fingers up the inside of my shirt, running my hands over my breasts as I go. I watch his eyes get big and can tell he's desperately trying to hold himself in check. He's dying to touch me. I pull my shirt over my head, followed by my tank top, and then slowly get up from his lap. Facing him, topless, I slowly undo the first button of my jeans, followed by the next. I shimmy my hips and glide my pants down, finally kicking them off completely. Standing before him in my underwear, I can see the desire burning brightly in his eyes.

Now it starts to get really interesting. I have him exactly where I want him, but I can tell his eagerness to touch me is going to just about do him in. I have a rule; there's no touching of my breasts allowed. I drag my thong down, ever so slowly, and step closer to him, standing there in all my nakedness. I drop to my knees and lean forward to unbuckle his pants. I take the opportunity to trail my hand firmly over the zipper as I undo it and his eyes roll back at the contact. He lifts his hips as I pull his jeans down, allowing me to slide them down the length of his legs and finally off over his feet. His boxer briefs are doing a poor job of containing his excitement, so I quickly relieve him of them and take a minute to admire him. His cock is standing firmly at attention just waiting for me to climb on.

His breathing is heavier, and I see his hands twitch towards me before he catches himself. I lean away and pick my jeans off of the floor to pull a condom out of the pocket.

"Do you always come prepared?" he asks.

I chuckle, "Always." I rip the condom open with my teeth and take stock of the 'toy' I get to play with, if only for a little while. He is big, there's no doubt about that, and I think I'm going to have some fun with him. I watch him watch me glide the condom down his shaft. His excitement is mounting and I can see in his eyes just how turned on he is. His dick twitches in my hand as I finish putting the condom on and stroke him gently a few times. I smile inwardly. He is totally under my control right now. This is the power I love, that I crave.

He's ready for me.

I stand up and climb back onto his lap, straddling his hips. He forgets my instructions from earlier and reaches forward to grab my breasts, but I stop him in midair, anticipating the move.

"No, my rules, my way." I say, moving his hands over his head. I lean forward and begin to gently slide down his length, running my tongue over his lips and into his mouth as I take him completely inside me. I don't even give him the chance to speak. Talking is way overrated, and I know exactly what he'd say, anyway, like déjà vu.

I continue to glide up and down, and as I hear his breathing increase I finally pick up the pace. I allow his hands to rest on each side of my waist. I feel his fingers dig into my skin, as he gets closer to letting go. I nip at his bottom lip before I lean back a little, applying pressure to create the sensation that will get me the release I sorely need.

"Yeah, just like that." I say and begin moving even faster. I'm so close to orgasm. The sensations become overwhelming and my body decides it's time to let go. The physical sensations and the control I have over the situation combine, and I am spiraling into bliss, feeling the relief and freedom that is not possible any other way. Joe follows quickly behind me, and the pulsing sensation as he comes extends my pleasure.

I don't know what it is about an orgasm that sets me free, but I feel it every time. I think it's being in control, and setting my own boundaries that I find freeing. I have such little control of anything in my life; this small piece of control keeps me from going insane. For just a brief moment, I'm deciding what I want and making it happen. I know the guys don't get my 'no touching' rule, but they don't need to. It makes perfect sense to me; it's too personal, too intimate. Some would say sex is far more intimate, but not to me. It's getting to know someone's body, taking the time to see what one likes or dislikes. Touching is far more intimate in my mind. Sex is just that, sex. I've never had it with someone I loved, so I don't know anything different.

I gather my clothes together, and turning to Joe, ask, "Where's your bathroom?"

He points me in the direction and tells me where the towels are. I nod thanks and go in, locking the door. I clean up and get dressed.

As I walk back into the living room, I notice Joe dressed only from the waist down.

"So, can I see you again?" he asks.

"I'm sorry, Joe, but this was a one-time thing. I don't have sex with someone more than once." I reply.

"So I'm good enough to have sex with, but not to date?" he asks, a little ticked off.

"It's not you, it's me. I know it sounds cliché, but it's the truth. It's just a rule I have, and I don't have time to date. I'm sorry."

"So you screw them, and then you leave them?" He doesn't say it unkindly, just matter of fact.

I sigh, "Look, you're a nice guy, and I'm sure you'll have no problem finding someone else. This was only ever sex, nothing more. No expectations. Just sex."

He looks away for a moment before glancing back my way. "I'm well aware the roles have been reversed here. I'm acting like a girl. I just don't normally do one-night stands, and I like you. I know we don't know each other, but there's just something about you I want to get to know better."

He's sweet; I'll give him that. I can't do this relationship thing, and even if I did, he's not someone I could see myself with. Don't get me wrong; he's nice. There's no denying that. Everything he's stated reinforces my perception that he's a good guy. I would ruin and taint that sweetness in a heartbeat, and I couldn't bear it. Unconsciously, pair of chocolate-brown eyes flash through my mind, followed quickly by the handsome face they belong to.

"I'm sorry. I really am. Call me a bitch, that's what I am."

He sighs, "You're not a bitch, and I'm not going to call you that. I'm just sorry you feel that way. " He smiles a small smile, "You're a cool chick, Ashley, and hot as hell." He says, shaking his head in memory.

"Thanks, Joe, and good luck. I've got to jet."

I leave him sitting there and move to the door, opening it and walking away. The moment it's shut I lean against the doorframe, breathing heavily. I'm surprised this even happened. I wasn't expecting this turn of events, and the truth of the matter is I *am* a bitch. I just hurt a perfectly good guy. What the hell is wrong with me? I'm so messed up and damaged. I'm no good for anyone, not even the best pair of chocolate-brown eyes I've seen, especially not him.

All of a sudden, the apartment door across the hall opens, and out walks the one person I was just thinking about. I'm sure my mouth resembles a frog trying to catch a fly; no doubt the shock is plastered across my face. Here I stand, with just a cami and jeans on, holding my shirt. I know what this looks like, and I feel my cheeks get hot.

Zeke…

Great, now I'm embarrassed.

"Ashley? Are you okay?"

I clear my throat and stutter a little, "Yeah, I'm fine. Do you live here?"

He looks me up and down, noticing my frazzled hair and the fact I'm holding my shirt in my hands. I'm glancing left and right, anywhere but at him.

"Ashley…"

He says my name with such reverence I can't avoid his gaze anymore. When I finally meet his eyes, there's a question in them. But before I can say anything, he puts two and two together.

"So, you know Joe? He's a nice guy."

My embarrassment reaches an all-time high. I watch Zeke watch me. He looks good. His converse, dark jeans and navy blue tee shirt. His hands are in his front pockets and he's rocking back and forth, clearly uncomfortable.

Nervous, I force myself to stop chewing on my lips and respond, looking anywhere but at him. I don't want to see the disappointment, or judgment.

"I just met Joe tonight."

"Ah, well, I won't keep you, then. I'll see you in class next week. Have a good rest of your night."

I finally glance back at him. I don't see any of the things I was expecting, only a tinge of sadness.

"Alright, see you next week."

CHAPTER 12

JUST FRIENDS

Zeke

I haven't been able to get Ashley out of my head. No matter how hard I try. It's like she's already made a place for herself in my heart. For whatever reason, I care. I can't explain it. I guess you could say I'm curious about her.

To say I was shocked beyond belief when I saw her, leaning against Joe's door, would be a grave understatement. At first, I thought something was wrong, but the more I watched her, the more I knew they weren't *just* friends. I noticed the embarrassment etched across her face, not to mention her avoidance of any eye contact.

I know people do it all the time; one-night stands. I've been there, and done that, but now I'm a grown man, and I can't do that shit anymore. I'm not judging her; it's just the thought of another guy's hands all over her makes my blood boil. I have no rights to her; hell, I don't even know her. Do I want to? *Hell yes!* But I can't. There are people depending on me to make something of myself. I have a responsibility to people I love, and they will always come first, no matter how badly I want something, or, more to the point, someone.

I know there's more to Ashley than meets the eye. She's intriguing and complicated. I sure as hell don't need any complications in my life, but I would love nothing more than to break down the wall she has up. I'd be lying if I said I didn't. I wonder, briefly, what my life would be like if I didn't have people counting on me. Don't mistake me. I love everyone I've left at home to be here, to make something of myself, with my whole heart. For a very brief moment, I take myself to a place I should never venture.

What it would be like to have Ashley in my arms; to see her laugh, and to kiss her until she's breathless, to touch every inch of her, and have my name cross her lips. It's a fantasy, not reality.

I shake myself out of the daydream and come back to reality, getting pissed at myself. I'm such a selfish bastard. My life is good, great even. I can't imagine not having the life I have now.

What would it hurt to be her friend? She looks like she could use one. Lord knows I could use one, too. Strictly platonic, friends only. As her friend, I could still try to make her laugh. I would just have to watch the boundaries, and myself.

Once again, I give myself the talk. Ashley and I will be lab partners, and it's okay to be friends. Why does it seem I'm doing an awful lot of convincing myself this is fine and will work?

Something in the back of my mind is screaming this won't work out the way I'm hoping, and *just* friends is going to be a hell of a lot harder than I think it will. But I shove it away and bury it down deep, for now.

Chapter 13

Excess baggage

I quickly walk out of the building and head to my car. Who knew the relief I'd feel just escaping to my car? I lock myself in and take my phone out to call Mac. I didn't even stay to look for her; I just needed to leave. I didn't want to run in to anyone. I feel my face catch on fire once again. Why do I feel so awful and bothered by this whole situation? I never would have cared what anyone thought about me before. I've also never been with a guy that wanted to date me after having sex. Or run into the guy that has been invading my mind.

I push the speed dial number that will take me directly to Mac. I need her like I've never needed anyone. I need someone to listen, and tell me I'm not crazy, or stupid, or whatever. The moment I hear her voice I instantly feel better. Like a cool blanket has wrapped around my burn. That's how I feel. Like I've been burned and the fire still needs to be put out. I'm a raging mess, and for the first time in my life, I have a true friend, one that listens without judgment, and doesn't require anything from me—a first.

"Hey Mac? Are you still here, or back at the apartment?"

"Nope, I'm still here. I waited for you, just I case it didn't take long." She teases.

"I'm in the car, can we go?"

"Of course," Mac says. "Ash, are you okay?"

"Yeah, I'll tell you when you get here."

"Okay, be there in just a second." Mac hangs up and it's less than minute later when she taps on the window. I unlock the door and let her in.

We drive back to our apartment in silence. She doesn't push; that's Mac.

In our apartment, I settle down on the couch and Mac sits opposite me.

"Where to start..." I begin. I clear my throat and begin my tale. "I was never a nice person in high school. I was horrible. I didn't think twice about making a move on other people's boyfriends, and I didn't care who I hurt in the process. I was in it for the challenge. It was a feeling of control, knowing I could take what wasn't mine. I didn't care about the end result. I just wanted what I wanted, and if someone else got hurt, I was okay with that. Let others feel the pain I'd felt. I knew what I was doing. The girls in school deemed me the 'evil bitch' and I was. You would have hated me.

"Mac, I was so embarrassed walking out of Joe's room. I've never felt like this before." I explain the behavior is not new to me, and I've never had a problem before now.

"Can I ask you questions? I won't judge you, Ash, you should know that by now."

"I know," I say. There's no condemnation on her face, or pity—nothing.

"How often do you get together with guys you don't know?"

I'm ashamed answering the question, but I trek on. "I guess as often as I can. Whenever I feel an itch, if you will." I look down, humiliated, as I begin. "It's the only form of control I have in my life. Let's face it, the Warden makes all of the decisions for me, and he doesn't trust me. Hell, he doesn't even love me." A single tear escapes and I wipe it away. "I'm not telling you this to make you feel sorry for me. It's the last thing I want."

"Ash, what happened to your mom? You've never talked about her."

I feel like I've been punched in the gut at the mere mention of my mom. I never talk about her ever, with anyone. The pain must be mirrored across my face because Mac begins to backtrack.

"You don't have to talk about her if you don't want to."

I shake my head, "No, I can't let it fester and eat at me anymore. I need to talk about it. It's been so long since I've spoken about her to anyone."

I think back and honestly can't remember ever talking about her to anyone, actually. I never spoke about her to Miranda; quite frankly, I didn't trust her as far as I could throw her. She would have laughed and taunted me, going so far as to say she probably didn't love me enough to stay, and she would've been right. My mother didn't love me enough to stay. I don't remember being loved, not since before my mom left. I recall the times she would read to me, or she'd laugh at something funny I'd said. I don't remember my parents being a happy couple. There always seemed to be an air of discord. I only recall my mom being happy when she and I were together. Until one day, she was just gone.

I swallow the tsunami of tears that want to break out. It's hard as hell and makes me choke, but I press on, hoping that maybe, just maybe, all this pent up shit I've been holding onto for so long will be replaced with relief. Relief from letting it go, if only just a little bit.

I turn away, escaping to another time and place. Remembering the past is hard, and I've always pushed it to the back of my mind. Taking a deep breath and exhaling, I begin.

"My dad hasn't always been so controlling. I do remember a time when there wasn't so much discord between him and my mom. His company took off, and he spent less and less time at home with us. He'd grown up with nothing, so being successful was a big deal to him. He never wanted to want for anything, or us, for that matter. The fighting between them got worse the more time my dad was gone. He was never home, and as a consequence, she became unhappy. She wanted out; he didn't want her to leave, and I'm sure he made it difficult for her."

Wistfully I say, "I loved my mom. We did things together and she was a good mom."

For a moment, a smile graces my face as I share the moments of my mom and her romance novels. The comfort of Jude Deveraux novels and how she would wind the story into a tale appropriate for her daughter to hear. "She would spend hours upon hours reading her books to me. It is the best memory I have of my mom."

"She sounds wonderful." Mac says.

"Yes she was, but then…then she left. I wasn't worth sticking around for. One day she was just gone. No goodbye, no nothing."

"What did your dad say about it?"

I laugh cynically, "All he said was mom couldn't live with us anymore, and I wouldn't be seeing her. That was it. No explanation, no goodbye, nothing. After that, I never saw her again. I think about her all the time, despite being left."

"What happened tonight, Ash, that had you so upset?"

"Here is where I tell you how even more messed up I am." I say, resigned, wiping my hands down my face. "The guy, Joe, he was a nice guy. I don't allow any guy to touch me. It's a rule. I take control. It's too intimate. We kiss, I'm on top and there is no foreplay. It's just my rules, a way to control the situation." I sigh, "He told me I was beautiful and we had sex. Sex was all it was supposed to be. He said he was interested in dating me. I was shocked, to say the least. I mean, who in their ever-loving mind would want to date a girl they just screwed? It was just sex. That's it. There were no expectations. What caught me off guard was that he was so nice. I'm not used to nice. I'm used to guys being okay with just screwing me and me leaving, and I'm good with that. It's all I have to offer. I can't do anything else. I'm the queen of mess-ups and I've made my share, trust me. I'm trying to do better and I have made some changes, but for the most part, I'm not a good person."

Mac interrupts me before I can continue. "Cut the crap, Ash! I can't sit here and listen to you bash yourself. I refuse to."

I'm surprised at her tone and look up at her. I just bared everything to her, okay not necessarily everything, but a lot of who I am.

She softens her tone. "I sympathize, and I'm sorry for everything you've been through. It hurts my heart to hear about your mom and dad. I knew something had to have hurt you, I just didn't know what. You haven't had it easy, especially not having your mom by your side, and feeling a sense of abandonment, which I can't even fathom. But, even after such a short period of time, I can tell you are a good person. Ashley, you have a lot more to offer than you think. You're more than just a good lay. We all have excess baggage, including me. Your parents do not define who you are as a person, that's your choice. You can choose not to change, or you can choose to become who you want to be. I see a woman who takes control in the bedroom, simply because it's the only form of control you have. Unless you choose to take back control in other parts of your life."

I stay silent and ponder what she's saying, and I see where she's going with this.

"Why have you never stood up and told your dad what your dreams are? Or what classes you want to take? Why do you let him call the shots?"

I know why. He's the only person I have left. Without him, I have no one, and I'll be left all alone.

"If I disappoint my dad, then I have no one."

Mac's face is filled with so much compassion. "Ash, but aren't you already alone? Haven't you been feeling alone all this time? I know it's hard, but what are you really losing by standing up for yourself, and telling him what you want out of life? What are you really losing? You aren't alone anymore, I'm here; and I always will be."

She lightens her tone, "You're stuck with me, now, and you can share my family with me. Trust me, they'll love you."

I'm stunned beyond words. I've never had anyone want me as I am. Knowing my faults and issues and still want me to be a part of their family. Tears finally make their escape, and for once, I don't hold them back. I need to let go, but there's still one more thing to get off my chest in order to let all of it go.

"There's one more thing." I begin. *Deep breath, deep breath.* "At the end of my senior year I was assaulted."

Mac gasps and her hand flies to her mouth.

"Fortunately for me, he didn't get a chance to finish what he'd started."

I will never forgive myself for not listening to Tori and heeding her warning.

"I'd been warned by a girl I later learned had been raped by the same guy that assaulted me. She warned me, and I was too stubborn to listen. In fact, it was her boyfriend who'd warned me."

I feel so awful about this next part and wince, turning away out of shame, I continue, "I'd even hit on her boyfriend during that time. I was trying desperately to get Will to sleep with me. I didn't like Tori, and she sure didn't like me, but for good reason. I never had a reason not to like Tori, except everyone always liked her and for that, I didn't."

I laugh coldly, "To say the least, my dad was not happy to be notified by the police officer of what had happened. He sent a driver to pick me up from the station. Of course, it was my fault. It was never spoken about again. I went to court by myself, and everything. I vowed that in college, things would be different and I could start over. I have rules now. I don't have sex with anyone with a girlfriend, and I refuse to be who I once was."

That's it, the last piece of me to tell. This is everything bad about me, and everything that has made me, me.

"Wow, Ash, do you know how brave you are?"

I'm shocked. "Me? I am not brave." I say shaking my head.

"Yes, you are. You went through that by yourself, and you're determined to change from the bitch you used to be. You've vowed to change the bad in your life and become better. That makes you brave!"

I never thought about it like that before and contemplate her words.

"Anybody can say they want to change, Ash. But saying it and doing it are two completely different things. From what you told me, you've already come a long way. What can we do to give you some control back in your life so you aren't seeking out random guys for sex? Because let's face it, you deserve so much more, whether you know it or not."

"Thank you, Mac." I say through the tears streaming down my face.

"Oh, and there's one more thing." I say. "Guess who lives next door to Joe."

Mac looks at me quizzically, having absolutely no clue. "I have no idea."

"Well, after I turned down nice guy Joe about dating, I let myself out. I was leaning against the door, trying to catch my breath, when who should walk out the apartment door? Zeke."

"You're kidding." she says.

"I wish; I was so embarrassed."

"Did he notice you and speak?" She asks.

"He noticed and spoke, all right. I'm sure I can just imagine what he must think of me now."

"See, you are changing. You care what he thinks about you. Don't be so hard on yourself. You don't know what he thinks. Don't make something there that isn't. I guess you'll see next class."

I hadn't thought about it like that, and she's right. I do care what he thinks, and I don't know why. I have no clue why this one particular guy makes me care, and makes me want to be seen as different. But I groan at the thought of seeing him in class. It excites me, but makes me nervous all at the same time.

We talk into the wee hours of the morning. I've never felt less alone than I do in this very moment.

Chapter 14

First impressions aren't always right

Ashley

I'm hoping last week with Professor Forrester was an anomaly, and I'm just imagining his interest. I get dressed and meet Mac in the kitchen, desperate to down some caffeine.

"Want to meet at the coffee shop before I head over to chemistry?"

"Yup, sounds like a plan, have fun."

"Bye," I throw out before I race out the door, hoping to get to class at a decent time and avoid any un-necessary attention.

I walk into class and see I made good time. The Professor is busy with a couple of girls blatantly throwing themselves at him. I've played this game before, and I can spot what they're doing from miles away. He's enjoying the attention, it's clear as day. I quickly look away, not wanting to be caught staring. That would completely suck.

"Hey, it's Ashley, isn't it?"

I nod my head. "Nick, right? Friends with Austin."

"You've got a good memory. I must have made an impression." He says.

I laugh, "Don't kid yourself." I say jokingly. "I'm good with names."

"I heard my man Austin flirted with you on your first day and his woman tore you a new one, but you held your own and handed his manhood right back to him. Nicely done," he says.

"I call it like I see it." I say. "I don't have time for that crap, and I don't have time to deal with jealous girlfriends."

"You handled yourself well, at least how Austin tells it."

I grin at up at him, "Thanks." Maybe he's not such a douche after all. It'd be nice to have a friend in here.

He plants himself in the seat next to me and we chat for a few minutes before Professor Forrester begins class. I notice right away when I'm spotted and he gives me the once over. My cheeks heat up and I know Nick notices it, as well. I quickly look away, trying to be nonchalant. It's like this throughout class. I listen and take notes, but I do not participate. Participating would be creating a dialogue with the Professor, and I can't do that. I don't want anyone to think I'm encouraging him. I'm avoiding all eye contact, but I can feel his eyes on me. I know when he's looking my way. I feel Nick look at me several times. I guess to see if I'm reciprocating or encouraging the attention. The moment class is over; I pack my things as quickly as I can.

"Wow, Forrester seems to have his sights on you" Nick smirks.

"I don't know what you're talking about." I say innocently, looking back down at my backpack.

"Don't give me that shit. You're hot, and you know it. You know when a guy has interest in you."

I glance up at him. "I'm not doing anything to encourage it." I say quickly. I don't need shit started, or a rumor, and I don't know Nick from Adam.

He puts his arms up as if to fend of my verbal assault. "Slow down, I didn't say you were." He begins seriously, "Just be careful of him." He leans in closer so no one hears, "I've heard rumors. If he wants something bad enough, he'll find a way. Just watch yourself."

My heart begins to speed up. This is disconcerting to say the least.

"Thanks for the warning, Nick. I appreciate it." I say. We walk out of the classroom together before I ask, "Why hasn't anyone reported him?"

"Have you seen the guy? The girls love him, and the guys aim to be him. He's a freaking Casanova. Do you think any of these girls would fend off his advances? These girls want him, they aren't going to report him."

"I'm just going to avoid him like the plague then."

Nick tilts his head at me. "Why aren't you enjoying his attention like all the other girls do?"

I think carefully before I answer. "I have no interest in screwing up my education, not for anyone. Not to mention, he's too old for me."

He throws his head back and laughs. "That's good to know, maybe then I've got a shot."

"Don't kid yourself," I say smiling. "But it's good to know you aren't the dick I first thought you to be." I wink.

He throws his hand over his heart like I've wounded him, but laughingly says, "Ah, that hurts me, woman."

He holds his hand out. "Friends?"

"Friends." I shake his hand, deciding to try out this friendship thing—you've got to start somewhere. "I've got to meet Mac at the coffee shop, want to come?"

"Sure, I love hanging out with hot chicks. Is Mac single?"

I shake my head, laughing, "You're impossible."

"Well, is she?"

I ignore the question, but we walk together chatting the entire way. I spot Mac at a table and see an eyebrow quirk up at seeing Nick with me. I make introductions and we settle at the table where Mac already has my coffee waiting for me. I snatch it up and look at her, "I love you." I chuckle.

"Ha ha, I know you do. I mean, how could you not?"

Nick takes off to go grab a drink of his own and Mac starts the twenty questions. I tell her as quickly as possible the short version about class and about the conversation he and I had.

Mac sits back in her seat with her mouth hanging wide open before saying, "Wow. Just wow. How does this happen. This is the last thing you need to be worried about. You have to do what Nick says and watch yourself."

I decide to change the subject, "Nick wants to know if you're single."

We share laughs and joke with Nick when he joins us again. It's easy and fun. As it turns out, Nick's not such a bad dude. He's funny, and he makes Mac and I laugh.

I feel my phone vibrate and I know what that means. It's the Warden, but this time—this time I choose to ignore it. This time is my time, and I'm not going to let him get to me. I don't look at it, I just leave it be. I see Mac watch me and smile when I put my phone back down. I'm learning, slowly, but surely.

I've got Mac and I'm making friends. This college thing is probably the best thing I could've ever done. I'll deal with the Warden later. Now, all I have to worry about is Chemistry. Oh yeah, and Zeke.

Chapter 15

Friends and Pissing off the Warden

I walk into chemistry with trepidation, not knowing what to expect from Zeke. How's he going to treat me? Is he going to think I'm a slut now? Will he look at me with such distaste that he'll ask for a new lab partner?

I slide into my seat and see him sitting next to it. He's staring at me, as if he was waiting for me to walk through the door. I'm a bit lost for words. I didn't expect to see him change seats and be seated next to mine when I walked in.

Surprising me, he introduces himself. "Hi, I'm Zeke, and I can be an ass sometimes. And you are?"

He's got a twinkle in his eye and this crooked grin you can't help but smile back at. "Ashley, and sometimes I'm a bitch."

He chuckles, "Well, that remains to be seen."

"Are you kidding?"

"I didn't exactly make it easy. How about we start with a clean slate. Friends?"

I don't even have to think about it; I want nothing more. "I'd really like that." I say, as genuinely as possible.

"Awesome," he says, rubbing his hands together, "Because we have a lot of work to do."

The rest of class flows seamlessly. We're given an assignment and half of class is a lecture, after which we work in pairs. Zeke hangs on every word the professor says. When we begin working together, he's professional, but witty. He still has a way about him that's comfortable to be around, and he explains when I don't understand the material. I understand a lot of it, but I have to work harder in this subject; it doesn't come to me as easily, and in the interest of our lab partnership, I share this with Zeke. He actually promises to help me any way he can to make sure I understand the material.

We walk out the door together when class is over. "Do you have class tomorrow?" he asks.

"No, tomorrow is my off day, where I spend it studying my butt off."

"Why don't we spend Tuesday's working on the chemistry project?" He hurries on, "It might help you understand the material better, if you want to?"

"No," I rush out. "I'd really like that." The excitement of him being in close proximity sends butterflies down to my core.

Lord, have mercy he has a nice smile.

"Awesome," he says and smiles. "Your place, or mine?" he asks. He emphasizes 'your place' and I get the feeling that's what he would prefer. I remember who lives next to him and quickly say my place. I certainly don't want to run into Joe.

He tries to catch it, but I see the look of relief. I think about it for just for a moment, wondering what it means. I decide to analyze it later, and we quickly set up a time for tomorrow. He begins walking backwards with this hundred watt smile I can't help smiling back at. He looks like a little kid in candy store.

"Until tomorrow?" He asks smiling.

"Tomorrow," I grin back.

He finally turns around, leaving me standing there. I just watch him walk away. I'm sure I look like a moron standing there, but I don't care.

I'm afraid just being friends with Zeke Whitman is going to be a hell of a lot harder than I think.

I feel my phone vibrate and I yank it out, hoping it will be Mac and not the Warden. Unfortunately, it's the latter. I know I have to answer this. I can't avoid him forever, no matter how much I'd like to.

"Hi, Dad."

"Why haven't you been answering my messages?" He barks.

"I've been busy with school, Dad." My voice wobbles with my uncertainty at what to say, and how to handle him. I'm scared, but I know he and I have to have a *come to Jesus* talk, and it needs to happen soon. Hopefully, I can put him off for as long as possible.

"Ashley, are you getting distracted by anyone? You seem distracted and not yourself."

If you mean a tall, dark-haired, brown-eyed boy that wears converse and glasses, then yeah.

"No, I've been doing all the work, and my classes are going well. In fact, I have a study group that starts tomorrow. Every Tuesday, in fact." He doesn't want to hear me tell him I'm doing well because he goes off. It's like he was itching for a fight.

"I don't want to hear you're doing things you shouldn't be doing. We certainly don't want a repeat performance of the end of your senior year. That was bad enough, and my company can't handle another scandal, especially, coming from the daughter of the President and CEO of the company. The stunt you pulled cost this company greatly. I have a reputation to uphold, and your tumble with that boy cost us. It would be good to remember that, if you think of doing something else stupid. Do you hear me?"

I'm dumbfounded and numb and cold all over. I feel like I'm being assaulted all over again. I feel myself walking backwards and I end up backing up to a bench, and I sit. My breathing picks up and I feel the tears coming. They can't be contained anymore. Tears fall, but then, all of a sudden, I feel a little bit of the fight come back into me. I'm so tired of being passive, and having the one person in my life, who should be there for me, put me down time and time again. Not to mention, claiming the assault was my fault. I know I should have listened and not been anywhere near that guy, but I didn't ask for it. I didn't ask to be held down against my will, to have my free will stripped away from me.

I hear the Warden continue to verbally assault me. My guess is because he didn't receive a response from me. I replay what I just said in my head. *He's verbally assaulting me.* My anger rises up a notch, and then I have an out of body experience. I say something I never ever dreamed of saying.

"Dad!" I holler into the phone. "I didn't ask for that situation to happen." I choke out. "I didn't deserve to have that happen to me; nobody does. I'm sorry." I quiet my voice a bit, noticing I'm getting some looks with my raised voice. "Dad, I'm working hard, doing all of my work, and I study during my off days. I don't know what else I can do to make you proud of me." I sniffle.

He's silent for a moment before replying, "Watch your tone, Ashley, and do not disrespect me. I expect you to answer the phone when I call. If I text you, then I demand a response. Do not disappoint me."

And with those last words, he's gone. I get up, knowing I just need to get home. I need my bed. I quickly make my way home. I hurry to my door, opening it as I hear, "Hey, Ashley, how's it going." I quickly try to put a smile on my face.

"Oh, hi, Austin, good. I'll talk to ya later, okay? I've got to do something."

"Are you okay? It looks like you've been crying. Do I need to pummel someone's ass for you?"

The thought of Austin kicking my dad's ass actually puts a smile on my face. "Thanks for asking, Austin, I appreciate it, but no thanks. I've got it taken care of." He nods his head and I walk through the door and into my sanctuary. I drop onto my bed, throwing the covers over my head.

He doesn't care about me, and he just proved it today. He's so concerned about his precious reputation, and he actually thinks what happened to me was my fault. I'd give anything, anything to have my mom. To have someone to go to and hold me, someone to wipe my tears and tell me everything is okay; someone who will stand up for me to my dad. As much I crave to have my mom be that person, she's not here, and hasn't been for years. That falls on me and me alone, and I decide, here and now, I have to do something about it.

This is my first year of college, and it's barely begun. Something has to give, if I'm going to make some changes. I sit up and wipe the tears from my face, grabbing my purse and yanking out my phone. I text Mac, asking where she is. Less than ten seconds later she replies she's almost home. Right after that, she asks if I'm okay. I reply that I will be.

Relief washes over me, and I realize how stunned I am that she is my go-to person. The person that I run things through, someone I know will always have my back. I never saw that as a possibility, ever, not with anyone. She's the one constant, and even though I haven't known her very long, sometimes…sometimes you just know. I've been around enough people to know sincerity when I see it. Mac doesn't have a bad bone in her body. She's the kind of person that when she cares, she cares all the way. Throwing one hundred percent in to every friendship. Every time I've told her something horrible I've done, she's never judged me. She let me start from scratch, and she doesn't see me as damaged. She sees me as someone worth giving her time to. She's my best friend. I say it out loud, testing the phrase out. It feels really good to say, and I smile as I say it again. Mac is someone who is with you for the long haul; she's proved it time, and time again.

I walk to the couch and sit, grabbing my legs and tucking them into me, wrapping my arms around them and wait for Mac. Barely two minutes later, she comes barreling through the door and throws her stuff down on the floor. She has a look of alarm on her face.

"What's wrong? Don't tell me nothing because I can tell." She sits down, crossing her legs in front of her and waits for me to explain.

I rest my case. This girl knows me better in just a couple of weeks than Miranda ever did, and I grew up with Miranda.

"The Warden called me and he was pissed."

Mac smirks, "Why? Because you didn't answer his text in a 'timely fashion'?" She uses air quotes when she speaks.

"Yes. That, and a couple of other things he brought up." I tell her the whole conversation, and I watch her face go from stoic, to angry, to royally pissed. She shakes her head when I tell her about the embarrassment my father felt over the 'indiscretion' he believes was my fault. I don't miss the *bastard* that escapes her mouth. When I finish, she sits back and says, "I'm proud of you, Ash, you didn't roll over. You handled yourself better than you ever have before. You didn't back down or remain submissive. You stood up for yourself. Now that is the Ash I know." She's quiet for a bit, deep in thought. Finally, she asks, "How far are you willing to go to gain some control of your life?"

"What do you mean?"

"You are stuck under his thumb in every way possible. Imagine if you could be free. Imagine if you had the capacity to show your dad you aren't going to back down, and you can be independent."

"How would I do that?" I ask curiously. I'm at the point where I will do just about anything to gain some control of my life. "What are you suggesting? Because I'm game for anything at this point."

"This is just a guess, but I have a feeling your dad probably paid the first year for your housing and tuition. Am I correct?"

I nod my head, confirming her suspicions.

"Excellent," she says, rubbing her hands together in excitement. This is what we are going to do. "We know you're safe this year, since he's already paid for your tuition and housing."

I begin to see where she's going with this, but let her continue.

"You can tell me no, Ash, the choice is yours, but if you want to get out from under his thumb, then you need to do something drastic to show him you mean business. Take his control away." She takes a deep breath and continues, "This also means being responsible and taking care of your tuition and housing yourself, no more of daddy's money. You will need to be financially responsible on your own. You know that's going to be the first thing he throws in your face."

I nod; she's right, he definitely will use it to try and control me. The funny thing is I have never cared about money. It's always been important to him, though.

"But you have time, Ash. You can begin to pull away slowly, but sophomore year, you need to be ready to have financial aid. Fill out every grant you can find to help pay for your college and housing. There are so many out there, and I know you'd qualify. I'm sure he had high expectations when you were in high school regarding your grades, right?"

"Are you kidding? He expected nothing less, he would have flayed me for sure." I say.

"Of that, I have no doubt," Mac says, smiling. "So hit him where it counts, below the belt, so to speak. Take care of yourself financially, and he can't control you through the money. Keep in mind he's sure to take your new car."

Truthfully, I never gave a damn about the car. The car was his idea, and it was all about impressions. He knows people here. What would it look like to have his precious daughter riding around in a less than stellar car? In his eyes that would look very bad. I never asked for it, so he can certainly have it back.

"I don't care about the car. I never did." I whisper quietly.

'You've got this, Ash. You have a whole year to confront him. He can't do anything except take your car away. Imagine how you will feel when you're able to take the classes you want to take. To be whom you want to be. What do you want to be when you grow up, Ash?"

It's a thought I have never entertained. Never in a million years. Who do I want to be? When I came here, I had resigned myself that this was my life and there was no changing it. That's what I had to look forward to. For the first time, I see a glimmer of hope, and it is all because of Mac.

I sheepishly look at her and say, "I couldn't do this without you. I would never have had the courage to do this without you."

"What are best friends for?" she laughs, but quickly turns serious again. "Actually, I don't believe that for a moment. I think you definitely would have taken the leap to separate yourself from your dad. Not now, probably, but eventually. I just think you needed a good friend to be there for you."

"A best friend," I say a little bit in awe. "I've never had one before."

"You do now, girl. I've got your back."

"I've never had anyone have my back before, either. They always wanted to talk shit about me, which I deserved." I hang my head in shame.

"From what you told me, you were a bitch, but you haven't been since I met you. You aren't that person anymore. Remember? This is the year of starting over. This is your new beginning."

A weight lifts off me, and I feel like a renewed person. Okay, maybe not renewed, but a better, more improved person. Someone I can actually like. Maybe someone worth loving, down the road. I'm not sure why, but my mind wanders to Zeke and then he's all I see.

"Earth to Ash." Mac giggles, moving her hands back in forth in front of my face. "Where did you go?"

I tell her about my new study buddy and that, beginning tomorrow, every Tuesday until the end of the semester we'll be working on our Chemistry project together.

"I think he likes you, girl."

I shake my head. "I don't know about that, he doesn't know me. I may not be his type." The possibility of Zeke liking me causes goose bumps to flare from my head, all the way down to my toes, causing me to shiver.

All I know is tomorrow I get to spend time with him, and I'm looking forward to it. But, first I want to try to be friends. Friends first? *What a novel concept.*

Mac and I spend the rest of the evening eating junk food, talking about guys and laughing. There's a lot of laughing. I don't feel the need to seek out a guy to have sex. I've certainly never felt so alive and in control.

Chapter 16

Strictly platonic

Zeke

Why do I have, what I'm sure is the dopiest, smile on my face? I'm excited, stoked really, at the prospect of being alone in the same room with Ashley. Nobody staring at her, because let's face it, that grates my last nerve. The moment she noticed me sitting next to her in Chemistry, her eyes were on me. She never glanced around, and for that moment, nobody else existed. After she sat down, I looked around and almost every guy had his eyes on her. I saw how they looked at her. Half of them had a look that said they want to throw her across their desk and have their way with her, right then and there. It makes me want to pound their faces in. I'm not normally so territorial, or violent, but I see in their eyes they only care about one thing. I don't think she even noticed it today.

I wanted to start over and, apparently, reintroducing myself to her was the ticket, because she smiled. God, that girl has such a nice smile and it lit her whole face up. She's gorgeous and there's a hell of a lot more to her than what she lets people see. First thing I noticed when we were talking was she is extremely intelligent. She doesn't give herself enough credit, though. I think she understands the material we're studying more than she thinks she does.

I was listening to the lecture, but kept getting distracted and would glance across at Ashley from time to time when she wasn't looking. Why does this girl get to me like she does? There's only ever been one person in my life that could distract me, but not to the same extent, never to this extent.

I continue to tell myself we'll just be friends and I'm okay with that, but truthfully, I don't know if I can be just friends with Ashley Davis. I don't know if I have that in me. I'm sure as hell going to try, though.

I get to my dorm and see Joe walking in at the same time. Joe tilts his head in greeting. "What's up, man?"

"Not much." Out of curiosity, I blurt, "So how do you know Ashley? I saw her coming out of your room on Saturday night." I'm such a fucking idiot. *Obvious much?*

He looks around a little uncomfortable, "I uh, just met her at the party that was downstairs. Why do you ask?"

"No reason. She's in a class of mine, so I was just curios."

"Okay, well I'll see you around."

"Oh, Joe?" My head is telling my mouth to shut up, but my mouth doesn't want to listen because I just have to know.

"Yeah?" he asks.

"Are you dating Ashley? I mean..." I'm such a dumb ass and decide to bang my head into the wall when I finally make it into my room.

Joe regards me for a moment. "No, man. I tried, but she wasn't interested. I liked her, and she's a good lay. A real good lay; the girl sure knows how to take charge." He laughs and I feel my hand go into a fist, ready to spring to life and connect with Joe's face. He says a little snidely,

"Granted, she didn't want me to touch her and had these 'rules' I had to abide by." He uses air quotes. "For a good time again, though, I'd go for another roll, even with her rules."

That's it, I'm done, and that's all it takes. I can't stand here and listen to him degrade her to my face. Not to mention the thought of his hands on Ashley makes me see red. *She's my friend. Right? That's why I'm ready to pound his face in? Yeah, that's it.*

I fly forward to punch the ever-living crap out of his face. I see the shock register on his face as he tries to block my punch. Fortunately, he's too slow, and I get him right in his left eye. His entire body falls backwards and he catches himself on the doorframe.

"What the fuck, man?"

I'm seething, "Here's the thing, you fucking dick, she's my friend and you don't talk about my friends that way. I thought you were a nice guy, but turns out, I was wrong. It's a good thing she turned you down. Look how you talk about her. She must have really good instincts, that's all I've got to say." My whole body is shaking, and I'm just waiting for him to give me a reason to attack again.

"Dude, I'm sorry." He hangs his head a little. "She may have bruised my ego a bit."

I shake my head at him as I open my door and head straight to my freezer, yanking out the ice tray and emptying it into a plastic zip lock bag. I sit on the edge of my bed, holding the bag on my knuckles. It's going to be worse tomorrow, but I'll be fine. I'll have to explain myself, but that's fine, too. I'll think of something.

I'm so pissed, but I think about everything he said. Her rules, and not touching? I'd be lying if I said I wasn't curious. But I'm trying to be friends, and really, isn't that all I have to offer? Friendship? She couldn't handle my responsibilities, or my life. I have no doubt she's definitely used to the finer things of life. There's no way I could ever give her those things. Hell, I'm late starting college. I should have started two years ago, but sometimes life doesn't work out the way you want it to. Sometimes you make monumental mistakes that come back to bite you in the ass. And as hard as they are, you step up and take responsibility.

As much as my head says stay away from Ashley, my heart says the opposite. There's an obvious chemistry that, quite frankly, can't be denied. I know she feels it, I can tell. But again, I can't give her the life she deserves. I have to keep it strictly platonic, no matter what my heart says.

I yank my phone out and realize the time; I need to call home soon. I miss my family.

Chapter 17

Sexy Water Bottle

I'm nervous. Several things roll around in my head—Zeke, my father, and yes, Zeke again. I briefly wonder what it would be like for Zeke to meet my dad. Truthfully, if he went in with an open mind, he'd probably like Zeke. But 'Mr. Davis' doesn't have it in him to like anyone, and would snub his nose at him in disdain. He'd take one look at Zeke's shaggy hair and Chuck Taylor's, and that would be all she wrote.

Mac left this morning with a knowing smile on her face. I quickly reminded her it needed to be kept as a friendship and nothing else. She'd looked at me curiously, but remained mum as she went out the door.

In typical girl fashion, I rushed around the apartment making sure everything was neat and tidy. I also looked in the mirror at least a half a dozen times. I've never been so concerned about my appearance, or dressed quite so carefully. I may have also gone to the market first thing this morning and picked up a few groceries for us to munch on. You know, just in case he got hungry.

I hear a knock on the door and I take one last glance in the mirror while commanding myself to chill.

"You've got this," I say mutter to myself. "Plus, this is not a date." I smooth my shirt and shorts and yank the door open.

Standing in the doorway is my friend Zeke, hot as ever. I say friend in my head as much as possible, trying to convince myself. He smiles big, and his eyes twinkle, and he looked good enough to eat.

Stop that!

"Hey," he says.

"Come on in." I notice his hand is wrapped up, and I know it wasn't like that yesterday. "What happened to your hand?"

"I did something stupid, and now, I'm paying the price. "It'll be fine in a couple of days. It's just a little sore."

He doesn't elaborate, and I don't ask. We aren't that good of friends, after all.

I point him in the direction of the table in the kitchen, where it would be best for us to work. He sits down and gets situated while I get my books and notes from my room. On my way back, I stop and watch him for a moment. He's gathering his notes, but he quickly looks up, as if sensing I'm there.

I rush in, pretending I didn't just get caught ogling.

I'm such an idiot. Real smooth.

I sit down and we begin working together. It's easy and not forced. He knows how to explain things to me so I understand them better. He's funny, and maybe a little brilliant. I like listening to him talk and his voice is soothing. It's comfortable.

As we are silently working on the individual portion of our project, I sense him looking at me. I glance up and see a look that doesn't look so friendly. It looks heated, but then it quickly falls away and is replaced with a friendly smile. "Can I grab something to drink?"

I get up and open the fridge, pulling out a bottle of water and hold it up. "This okay? Or I have soda?"

"Water would be great, thanks."

I hand him the water and our fingers graze. Electricity, like nothing I've ever felt, passes through me and takes me by surprise. I quickly glance up and see him looking down.

Okay, must have been just me.

We continue working, but I can't help the disappointment I feel, knowing I'm the only one that felt the spark, but I tell myself to shrug it off and get a grip.

"So," he says breaking the silence. "What do you do for fun around here?"

"I usually hang out with Mac."

Yeah, when you're not trying to screw some random guy.

I dismiss the thought entirely, knowing that I'm trying to change this part of me, along with several other things.

"Mac?" he asks. "You live with a guy?"

I throw my head back and laugh. I never imagined anyone would think I was talking about a guy, she's just Mac.

"What's so funny?" his lips do that cute half smirk and I can't take my eyes off them for a moment.

"Mac is short for Mackenzie," I explain.

A look of relief quickly washes over his face. "Well, what do you and Mac do for fun around here?"

"Mac and I go to parties and go dancing. I love to dance." I say, a little too dreamily.

He tilts his head to the side. "Are you sure you aren't taking the wrong classes?"

"What do you mean?" I ask surprised at the question.

"When you said you liked to dance you got this look on your face. Are you any good?"

"I'm alright," I drag out.

He looks at me. I mean he *looks* at me, like he can see inside my soul. "I guarantee you're more than all right. Something tells me you're pretty damn good."

I can't help the blush that rises up. Now I'm curious and I have to know. "Why do you say that?"

"Your eyes twinkled when you mentioned dancing."

"Really," I tease. "You noticed that?"

"I'm a pretty observant guy, and I notice things," he says tapping his head.

"You are, are you?" I laugh.

"I am," he says with that same half smile.

For a moment there's just silence and we're staring at each other, grinning like fools.

Zeke clears his throat, breaking the spell, and asks, "Do you ever go dancing other than the weekend?"

"We haven't yet. We're usually pretty nerdy during the week. We spend it inside, studying."

"You? Nerdy? Never!" he chuckles. "It's too bad." He begins. "I'm not normally around during the weekends, and I'd love to see you dance sometime."

My stomach flutters at the thought of going dancing with him, and of him watching me dance.

God, the show I'd put on for him…

My head rewinds to the part where he's never around on the weekends. "Where do you go on the weekends?" I ask curiously.

A look crosses his face briefly before his expression smoothes out again. If I hadn't been watching him so closely, I would have missed it.

He runs his hand through his thick, dark hair, causing a lock to fall into his face and averts his eyes away from me. "I have family that needs my help on the weekends, and I kinda miss them when I'm gone." He turns back, looking me directly in the eyes, and smiles. "You must think I'm a pansy ass for going home every weekend."

Pansy ass was not what I was thinking; no. I was thinking the complete opposite. I'm thinking this guy, who already seems so perfect, just got a little more perfect. You never see guys that love and miss their family so much that they return home every single weekend. When I respond, I don't dare look him in the eyes. I'm afraid every feeling and thought I just had for him would be revealed on my face. That can't happen. I'm supposed to be friends with him, nothing more. Just friends. I try as best I can to wipe any and all traces of emotion from my face. I glance down at my hands, rubbing them together, and finally look up. I look at him, but remind myself to avoid the eyes.

"No, I was thinking the opposite. I think it's great you have such an awesome relationship with your family. Most of us would kill to have that." I say wistfully.

"I'm glad to hear that," he says seriously. A look of pure desire encases his face, and if I wasn't trying to be just friends with him, I'd climb over the table and throw myself at him like an animal in heat. But I don't. I refrain, and it's one of the hardest things I've ever done.

I quickly jump up to keep myself from becoming a woman in heat, and busy myself by grabbing another bottle of water out of the refrigerator. I open it and drink several large gulps, using my arms to wipe the excess off of my lips. When I set my water down, I notice Zeke staring at me. And what he says is nearly my undoing.

"I've never, in my life, wanted to be a bottle of water...until now."

I think my mouth opens. My heart is beating a million miles a minute and my skin is on fire. I feel a pull towards him I can't explain. I can't move; I'm frozen in place. He walks towards me and raises his hand to my mouth and traces my lips with his thumb.

"Such pretty lips."

I don't move, I can't. But my mouth finally finds words. "We're friends, right?"

His eyes swirl with emotion, and I see him fighting something internally when he takes a step back and lowers his hand. "You're right, I'm sorry. I shouldn't have done that. That was highly inappropriate of me, and certainly not fair to you."

I try to talk, but he interrupts me. "Ashley, it won't happen again, and if you feel uncomfortable around me, you can change partners. We can also go the library if you'd feel better being around other people—" His comment destroys me, "It won't happen again."

"Stop." I say quietly, but with enough force that he gets the point. "Its fine, but maybe the library wouldn't be a bad idea?" I offer a lopsided grin, because quite frankly, it's all I've got in me, and I don't want him to see the disappointment. I can act with the best if I have to. Hell, I've been doing it my whole life.

"I should go." He begins to pack his things and stands, ready to walk out the door.

Before the door closes I spit out, "Maybe we could get a group together and go dancing one night this week, or next, during the week. You know…if you want to?"

Yeah, I'm playing with fire here and risking getting my heart broken.

"You'd break your weekly routine for little old me?" he smiles.

"It's time I break some old patterns in my life and live a little, I deserve it."

He chuckles, "I don't doubt it for a minute. You let me know when and where, and I'll be there. I wouldn't miss seeing you dance." He winks and then the door closes, leaving me breathless and hot as hell everywhere. I have an ache that needs to be filled, but I'm afraid the only person that could ease it just went out the door.

CHAPTER 18

BLUE BALLS

Zeke

I couldn't get out of there fast enough. If I didn't, I was going to strip her naked and take her, right then and there, on the kitchen table, and last time I checked, that's not what friends do. The moment the door shuts, I readjust myself. My dick is packed like sardines in my pants and I need relief, but sadly that's sure as shit not in the cards for me. The only person that could quench this need is the one I just walked out on.

I don't know what's wrong with me. When I started college, I told myself I wouldn't let this happen. That I wouldn't get involved with anyone. I have nothing to offer anyone. I think about the last serious relationship I had, and it sure didn't happen the way it was supposed to. She's long gone now and never looked back. It's a crying shame, too, the things she's missed out on.

I'm frustrated, and I'm not just talking sexually. Not even since my last relationship have I ever felt so drawn to someone. Her smile is contagious, and the things I see in her eyes that haunt her, I want to make better. I want to know everything about her, and I certainly want to see those long legs of hers dance. The problem is she deserves a hell of a lot more than I can give her. God, if she only knew the responsibilities I carry. It'd be a turn off for any girl to handle. How could I ask it of her? The answer is, I can't.

I'll have to be the guy that is just friends with the girl he likes a lot, and watch while she dates other guys. I'll be like the gay best friend, only I'm not gay. The thought of seeing her date anyone pisses me off. But that's just the way it has to be.

I drive to my apartment as quickly as possible. Thinking about Ashley the entire way isn't helping my already throbbing dick. I hurry into my dorm, grab my clothes and take them into the bathroom. I need a shower, pronto, and have a need to take care of.

I strip down; turn on the faucet, warming the water. I slide in, leaning my head forward and let the water cascade over me. Ashley's face is all I see, drinking from that damn bottle of water. I grab my cock and start stroking it, picturing Ashley's small soft hands gripping me, and stroking me into oblivion. Staring at the tile, my focus is only on her beautiful face...The more I focus on her lips and her eyes, the faster and harder I grip myself. I picture myself grabbing her and laying her across that kitchen table of hers and burying my face in that sweet spot between her legs. I can almost taste her as I continue to stroke...and that's when I lose it. The more I see Ashley, the harder it's going to be for me. Literally.

CHAPTER 19

A FRIEND HE'LL STAY

After Zeke leaves, I attempt to calm my raging hormones and decide to go on a run. Running is something I've always loved; I just haven't done it in a long time. I throw my running clothes on, pull my long hair into a ponytail, and lock the door on my way out. I spot Austin as I walk down the hallway, in a heated argument with his bitchy girlfriend. I ignore them, but hear Austin tell me hello as I pass. Out of the corner of my eye, I see her slap his arm. I can't help the chuckle that escapes my mouth and shake my head. I don't want that kind of relationship. As I open the double doors Nick comes walking in.

I immediately try to stop him. "Are you going to see Austin? Because if you are, just know he and his bitchy girlfriend are in a pretty heated discussion."

"Ah, they're at it again, I see." He waits a beat before saying, "Nope, don't care and gets a devilish grin on his face." I hear him grumble, "Bitch lady," as he heads back in. I chuckle and think what a character he is.

I begin stretching my legs. I'll probably kill myself since it's been so long since I've gone for a run. But I need it and this is possibly the only thing that will calm me down.

Except for the real thing.

I start off slow, building momentum, and it's not long before I'm back in my running groove. I love the familiar burn of my calves and my stomach clenching with each pump of my arms. I pass students here and there, catching looks out of the corner of my eye from several male students. I used to love those looks, even get high off of them, but not anymore.

No, now there's only one person I'd like to have eyes on me. Unfortunately, he doesn't seem to want me.

I replay his quick retreat. I know we said we'd start over and be friends, but what if I want more, or crave more?

He seems pretty determined about staying only friends. A friend he wants, a friend he'll get. I'm not playing any games anymore, but I'm sure as shit not going to keep this up. Normal girls date, right? Maybe that's what I need to do. Maybe in order to get my *friend* Zeke off of my mind, I need to see what's out there.

I continue along the edge of campus and follow along the walkway that leads to another area for joggers. I look around as I do and note what a beautiful campus it truly is. I've never taken the time to notice before. They've built a pretty sweet area for joggers and I notice I'm not the only one craving a run.

I see several staff members, as well as a slew of students, that look familiar. I decide this could be a good place to meet someone, and I should bring Mac next time. I need to find Mac a good guy, someone that's good enough for her.

It isn't long before Zeke creeps back into my head, and I'm internally cursing myself for once again thinking about him. I push myself harder, running at a speed that is sure to leave me breathless. He invades my mind, and that's when I realize it's not only my mind he's invaded, but my heart, as well. Why?

I realize, no matter how hard I run, there's no escaping my feelings. I'll do as planned. If I want him in my life, then a friend he will stay.

Chapter 20

I'll take what I can get

The week flies by, as does the weekend. Classes are routine, and I continue to study my ass off. I need to keep my grades up in order to apply for grants and scholarships. I also didn't see Zeke again, but I knew he'd be gone for the weekend. Mac and I don't go anywhere, we stay in and watch movies and chat with some of our surrounding neighbors. Nick is there, hanging with Austin and a couple of others, so we invited them to come watch movies with us. Nick and a guy named Ian. Poor Austin wasn't allowed. Nick said his girlfriend would have beaten his ass if she found out. I am completely unsurprised. I certainly don't want to be in her line of fire.

Nick kept us laughing the entire time with his commentary, while Ian added to his comedy routine. Funny guys, and I think Nick may have a thing for Mac. He sure was doing a lot of staring.

It was nice to hang out with a group of guys as friends and nothing more. No jumping their bones; just a couple of guys, hanging out with a couple of girls, watching movies. I realize this is the first weekend I haven't gone dancing and hooked up since I school started. I don't feel the itch I normally feel.

I didn't have a lot of contact with the Warden. He texted and I answered. I have a plan in place, so the pressure has been removed. I give him deadpan responses, no emotion attached. He doesn't show any either, though, but I don't care anymore. The heavy weight of him hounding me, and the worry about what I will say to him has been removed, especially the sensation of my stomach dropping at the vibration of my phone. Now, I tell him what he wants to hear.

English class goes without a hitch, but I think it helps having Nick in my class. He helps keep Forrester on his toes. I catch the looks and his wandering eyes, but other than that, it seems he's left me alone since I have a friend in class with me. Thank God for Nick. Those are words I never thought I'd say out loud.

Chemistry is that, chemistry. It's what I feel every time I'm around Zeke. It's instantaneous. It could be anything from him barely glancing at me, a nod of his head, or a crooked smile to his gorgeous lips. I swear I can feel his body heat coming off of him in droves right beside me. He's patient and sweet, and nothing is ever mentioned of our close encounter.

When we meet at the library to study, it's all work. But I lose myself when he talks, and he switches from serious to his trademark crooked smile in a nanosecond, his eyes dancing when he laughs. I lose myself in him so easily, but have to keep reminding myself we're friends, which is better than nothing at all. I'll take what I can get.

I notice more about him than a friend should. I notice his hands and how large they are, and picture them being wrapped around my waist, or pulling me close. I've had dreams about him using those fingers in other ways. I woke one night in a pool of sweat; so hot for him I couldn't go to sleep until I calmed the fire raging inside me. I closed my eyes and pretended my hands were his. I slowly slid my hands down my stomach and into my panties. I found myself soaking wet as I slowly circled my finger around my clit before sliding it inside of me. I heard myself moan, but all I saw and felt was Zeke. It wasn't my fingers inside of me; it was his. I used my other hand to gently cup my left breast and circled and lightly pinched my sensitive nipple between my thumb and forefinger. In my mind, his mouth was sucking and lightly biting it, and he was sending me to a place I've never been. The more I thought about Zeke, the faster and deeper my finger went and the harder I pinched my nipple. It wasn't long before I reached climax, and as I did, Zeke's name passed my lips. I lay there, thrumming from the pleasure of my self-induced orgasm letting my mind wander. It didn't escape me that the two things I fantasized about Zeke doing to me, I have never allowed anyone else to do.

The next three weeks feel as if I am stuck on repeat: I go to class, study, sleep, waking up and fantasizing Zeke is doing naughty things to me, while having absolutely no time for actual fun. Mac and I are hitting it hard with the books and spend most of our time studying in the evenings. We even turned down a movie night with Nick and Ian.

The Warden called me one night. I didn't yes sir and no sir him the entire time either. I held my own. Mac was there, cheering me on with a thumb's up. I wasn't disrespectful, but I wasn't a mouse either. There was a lot of irritation in his voice, but I didn't back down like I usually would've.

I have an appointment with a financial aid advisor next week that I'm a little worried about. I want everything kept on the down low. I don't want my dad to catch wind of my plans. Getting out from under his thumb is proving difficult. He knows a lot of people, and I know he has spies watching me. He has said as much. It takes time to hear back from grants and scholarships, and I don't want to wait until the last minute; otherwise, I could be screwed. I have to be ready for next year, which seems so far away, yet it's not.

CHAPTER 21

ALL THINGS ASHLEY

Zeke

I lay in my bed, replaying the past few weeks, man have they been rough. Classes are going well, and I love spending time with Ashley, even if it is just studying. She's kind, sweet, and funny; talks about Mac all of the time, and how much fun they have together, just doing absolutely nothing. She's opened up a little. I know her dad's basically a dick. She hasn't said a lot, but enough for me to get the gist.

I'll say something to make her laugh and she'll throw her head back, making my cock twitch. I guess I love punishing myself. She just has that effect on me.

Every single night I've spent with my hand getting reacquainted with my dick. All I do is picture her face and luscious lips and I'm a goner. I want so much more than friendship, though. I want her, all of her, in every way. I know she has things she doesn't let spill; so do I. How do I get over this and let go? Every day I question why we continue to stay friends, when all I want is to have so much more with her. But as soon as I question myself, I'm quickly reminded why. She's not the kind of girl that could handle my life, and the reality of it is, despite how hard it's been, I wouldn't change it for the world. A few years ago, it was rough. I'm not sure if rough is even the right world.

Challenging? Hell yes. But what I got in the end is more precious than I could ever have imagined.

Every time we're together in class, or at the library, I want to hold her hand. I feel this possessive need to make sure everyone knows she's mine. I'm not an idiot. I see the looks, the stares when she walks by, and the overt looks directed at inappropriate places where they shouldn't be staring. I've even caught myself on the verge of growling. Not just one time, but several times.

While my mind is wandering in dirty places involving all things Ashley, I receive a text.

Ashley: Hey, Z, we've been working so hard, I need a break. You in?

Me: What do you have in mind?

Ashley: Night Club, Thursday at 9:00? :D

It doesn't even take me a second to give her an answer. I mean really? This means I get to see her dance.

Me: I'll be there.

Ashley: See you then.

I throw my arm over my eyes, sighing.

Shit.

Once again, like a horny teenager, I picture Ashley seductively swinging her hips from side to side, with a come hither smile brightening her face. She has eyes for me, and only me. She crooks her finger at me, wanting me to join her.

I groan out loud, shaking my head. I've got to get a grip on my hormones. I can't hurt her. Honestly, I'm afraid I'm going to be the one getting hurt. It may be a little too late for me.

CHAPTER 22

ALIVE

I lay on the couch waiting for Mac to get home when I decide I'm in need of some fun. We deserve fun, dammit. We've been working nonstop and one night isn't going to kill us. I'm restless and running isn't going to help. My body needs—no it craves—to dance.

I'm not sure what comes over me to text Zeke; my fingers have a mind of their own. I justify it by saying he did want to come the next time we went out. I'm just being a good friend.

Sure Ash, keep telling yourself that.

I throw a pillow over my face and scream. I scream for my frustration, and for the guy I so desperately want. The guy that treats me with respect and makes me laugh; the only guy I've ever craved to touch me all over. I'm still screaming into the pillow when I hear the front door open.

"What did that pillow ever do to you?" Mac smirks, tossing her bag onto the floor.

"I may, or may not, have made plans for us to go dancing Thursday night and invited Zeke." I cringe when I say the last part.

"It's about damn time! You two have been skirting around each other for weeks."

"It's not that simple, Mac."

"Why isn't it? He likes you."

"You don't really know that, and he's made it pretty clear we're to stay friends." I cringe when I say friends. The word puts a sour taste in my mouth every time I think it.

She taps her chin with her finger. Something she does when she's thinking. It's a Mac "thing".

"No, he likes you. I know it. The question is why is he fighting it?" She perks up. "This will be good for you. Ooh, I get to observe you." She claps her hands in excitement. "I'll ask the guys if they want to come. It'll be fun to have a group of us."

I eagerly agree to the idea. "It'll be fun. I really needed a night out, too."

She yanks her phone out and texts Nick and Ian.

"While we're on the subject of guys. What's going on between you and Nick?" I ask.

She quickly glances up and has a slight blush. "Nothing. We're friends, that's all. Not to say he isn't hot, he is. He's just a funny guy." She shrugs her shoulders, as if that explains it all.

He is pretty damn funny, and a flirt to boot, but it's innocent. Ian's sweet, too. We recently learned he has a girlfriend named Ryann, back home, that he's very attached and loyal to. It's sweet, and makes me want that, as well. I'm envious of their relationship and trust. He'd called her one night and put her on speakerphone. He'd said we were good girls and she had nothing to worry about. She'd laughed and ended the call with telling us to take care of her guy. I couldn't begin to fathom the amount of trust these two have for each other. I'd sat there, deep in thought, remembering the old me, and how horrid I used to be. I wouldn't have ever cared that someone was taken, and would have hurt them both.

"Okay, the guys are in. Nick is going to see if Austin wants to come. He said he needs a break from his bitchy woman."

"Do you find it odd we don't have any other female friends?" I ask.

Mac smirks, "Um, not really. I have some female friends in my classes, but they've never expressed any interest in being friends outside of class. I guess I've never thought about it. I'm sure one day we'll expand the female population in our group, but for the time being, it's kind of nice being the only girls. Don't you think?"

I have to admit it's been so easy being friends with these guys. There's no drama, and it's simple. You know where you stand. Maybe except for one...

"Agreed." I quickly reply

"I'm so excited to go out. You never know, I may run into my dream man." She laughs.

"You never know," I reply. "Stranger things have happened."

As I lay in bed, tossing and turning, I vow that Thursday, regardless of what lines Zeke has drawn, I'm crossing them. I want to see where this can go. I want to take this monumental leap, and put myself out there. I've never pictured myself with anyone, but as crazy as it sounds, I can see myself with him. I can't describe the want and need I feel for him. He's everything I've ever wanted. There's never been anyone to make me feel. Make me feel special, like I'm worth something. For the first time ever, I feel like I have something to offer someone, and I feel alive.

CHAPTER 23

THANK THE LORD ABOVE FOR FRIENDS

Thursday night couldn't get here fast enough. I'm giddy as hell, and I've been looking forward to a night out. Mac is just as excited. We've been cooped up in this apartment for a month, which is more than long enough, and we deserve a night out.

I holler for Mac and sit down on the corner of my bed, feeling dejected. She comes rushing in. "What's wrong?"

Chewing on my lip, I confess, "I don't know what to wear. What do I wear tonight? I just don't know. I have to look good, Mac. I have to look smokin' hot!" I rush out.

"Slow down, girl, I'll help you. Plus, don't you realize he's going to like whatever you wear?"

"Um, no." I grumble out.

"Everywhere you go, guys check you out. You could wear a paper sack and they'd still stare at you. Why are you so dang worried?"

I look everywhere but at her and quietly say, "I'm going to make a move on him, and I want to make sure I have his full attention."

Mac sits down beside me, "Ash, if he likes you as much as I think he does, from everything you've told me, I think you're going to be just fine."

"I'm so damn nervous."

Mac gets up and starts flipping through my clothes in the closet. "Do you want me to help you decide what to wear?"

"Help me not look like a whore, but still look hot. Shit, I've never worried about this before."

"That's because you've never liked anyone enough to care."

She's right; I haven't. It's like a light bulb goes off and I get it. It finally dawns on me, and I'm beginning to understand my fucked up behavior, little by little. Every guy I went out with, I screwed, and that's all they ever were to me; a screw. They were a conquest. It was something to make me feel better about myself, if only for a little while—a power trip. I don't like that about me. It's one more thing to make sure I never repeat. The next guy I'm with, I'm going to care about.

"You're right," I say looking up at her. "So help me find something to look great in, where I'll knock his socks off."

She pulls a pair of tight skinny jeans out of my drawer and pairs it with a fitted black tank. She then pulls a pair of red sequined heels out of my closet.

"Can you wear these while you're dancing?"

"Girl, I can dance in anything. Good choice by the way. Straight or wavy?" I ask pointing to my hair."

"Wavy, it's more you."

"Thanks, Mac," I say sincerely. She has no idea everything she's done for me, and I will always be grateful to her.

I grab my clothes and head to my bathroom to shower and get ready. It's hard to contain my excitement. As I'm putting on the finishing touches of my makeup, I see Mac walk in and lean against the doorframe.

"Looking good, girl," She says. The moment it's out of her mouth there's a knock on the door. I take one last glance in the mirror before heading into the living room with Mac. I'm not the only one dressed to impress. Mac's on the shorter side, but she's wearing heels and skinny jeans also. Instead of a tight shirt, she's wearing a camisole under a slinky chiffon shirt that hangs off of one shoulder. Sexy, but understated. She opens the door and I see Nick, Austin, and Ian all hovering in the doorway. They are all good looking guys, but so different. Austin has the typical all-American looks with his blond hair, and very muscular build. Nick is tall and a little thinner with short-cropped dark hair and always has a flipping smile on his face. Behind his back we call him the Italian stallion. Then there's unavailable Ian. He's more muscular and nearly bald since he keeps his hair shaved so short. He's got a dimple on one cheek when he smiles. His girlfriend Ryann is very lucky.

Nick places his fist at his mouth biting down lightly on it and says, "Mmmhhhh, you both look good enough to eat."

Mac blushes and I just shake my head, smiling. This is Nick. He throws his arm over her shoulder giving her a quick squeeze.

I turn to Austin, "So Austin, how did you get cut loose tonight? I didn't think your girlfriend would approve, especially without her coming, too." I ask, smirking.

He looks up sheepishly before looking away. "She'll get over it, she always does."

That's the end of that topic. I can sense he doesn't want to talk about it, and I'm certainly not one to push, not anymore. I've learned when to shut up.

My phone buzzes and I'm afraid to look down, but I do because it could be Zeke. I don't want the Warden ruining my mood for the night. Fortunately, it is Zeke and relief courses through my body. I read the text and quickly respond back.

"Zeke will meet us there, he's running behind."

They all look at me simultaneously. "Who's this Zeke guy?"

Mac laughs, "Down boys. It's Ash's lab partner and friend."

"Is he the reason you wouldn't go out with me?" It seems Nick is only half joking and I don't know how to answer. Thank goodness Mac saves me.

"Nick, you're such a goob. We'd hate to ruin our friendship by dating you."

Nick looks dejected. "Yeah, but we weren't friends at that point. Can't we just be friends with benefits?" Finally he smiles, teasing.

"You're such a shit head," Mac says, smacking Nick on the arm. Meanwhile, I'm standing there, listening to them banter back and forth, thinking how lucky I am. As different as we all are, I'm grateful for them.

These are my friends.

"Let's go, I'm ready to let loose. I've been holed up in this apartment for what seems like forever."

As we make our way, I get the feeling that everything is going to change tonight and will never be the same.

CHAPTER 24

A NIGHT OF FIRSTS

Zeke

I'm freaked out about tonight. Not a bad freak, a good one. I'm uncertain about what the night holds in store. This trying to stay friend's thing is for the fucking birds. Why must my head and heart be on opposite sides of one another?

Ashley had told me she'd be going with a group of friends, and I'm anxious. Not about the friends, but about how my body's going to react to seeing her dance. If all she has to do is talk to make to me hard, imagine what dancing will do to me. I run my hands through my hair, readjust myself because I've already given myself a semi-hard on just thinking about it, and start my way over to the club.

I walk in and hand the guy my I.D. Club Z is an eighteen and over club, but since I'm over twenty-one, I get a special bracelet to wear. I just turned twenty-one last September. It dawns on me that Ashley and I have never discussed age. *Shit.*

Hopefully, it won't be much of an issue. I head over to the bar and grab a beer. I need something to calm my racing heart. I smile at the bartender, who's attempting to get her flirt on, grab my beer and turn around, not missing

137

the look of disappointment that crosses her face. I take in the bodies bumping and grinding on the dance floor and swig my beer down.

Like a homing beacon, I find her. She's staring at me intently, as if she was waiting for me. Smiling, she begins to head my way when a hand grabs her arm, stopping her. It sets me on high alert, and I quickly make my way to her. I see her turn to the person, smile at them and say something. When I reach her, I'm fuming internally.

"Hey," she says.

I glance at the guy's hand that's still on her arm, following it up to his face. He's smirking like he's enjoying this and giving me a stare down. He finally nods his head at me.

"You must be Zeke."

I smirk back. He doesn't intimidate me one bit. "I am, and you are?"

"Austin, I'm a friend of Ashley's."

Ashley scoots closer to me and stares at Austin, finally saying, "Knock off the pissing contest, Austin."

He smiles at her and finally cackles, "Just watching out for you, babe."

Ashley shakes her head, ignoring him, and begins making introductions. "This is my best friend and roommate, Mac. Next is Nick, and this is Ian."

I barely acknowledge everyone when she leans up and whispers, "Let's dance." She has this gleam in her eye. She's excited and seems carefree tonight. I like this carefree side of Ashley. She grabs onto my arm, sliding her hand down it and into my hand. Hands linked, she pulls me onto the dance floor. She doesn't have to pull too hard; I'm more than willing to follow her anywhere.

I'm holding her hand and standing in the middle of the dance floor. Her eyes widen in surprise when I spin her around, pulling her back to my front, and draping her arm around my neck, she lets go of my hand as I rest my other hand on her hip. I'm completely engulfed in all things Ashley. She tightens her hands around my neck and begins playing with the hair at the nape of my neck. If she only knew what this does to me. She begins swaying her hips, rubbing her ass up and down my cock. It doesn't take long to make me hard. No way. Not with Ashley. I let her lead because she's the dancer, plus I'll follow wherever she takes me. I'm a goner now. Just having her ass rub me is enough to be my undoing, and I know she can feel how hard I am for her. I follow her moves, but just as quickly as I turned her around, she turns around on me. We're now dancing face to face. Her eyes are playful and shining. I slide my knee between her legs and follow the beat of the music. I'm playing with fire, and for once I don't give a shit. I'm in the here and now, living in the moment where I have no responsibilities. I'm just a twenty-one year-old guy, out with the girl he likes a lot.

Her face is soft and carefree and the song changes to a sexier, slower tempo. She slithers as close as she can and with each beat of the music, her pussy hits my leg. Her eyes grow big and she tightens her arms around my neck, once again running her hands through the nape of my hair. With each rub on my leg, my hand tightens around her waist. I see her lips part every time the friction hits her just right, and I see ecstasy building in her angelic face. Her dance moves are fluid and never miss a beat. She tightens her hands once more and I feel her nails begin to dig into my neck. It's not painful, not by a long shot. She's close; I can feel it. Her eyes are half lit and I hear her whisper my name. This makes me want to give her everything. Hearing my name leave her lips causes a shudder to race through me. I lean forward and whisper, "Let go."

She stares up at me with no inhibitions, no concern and rubs herself on my leg one last time before letting go. It's the sexiest thing I've ever seen. I swoop in and grab her lips with mine, muffling her heavy breathing and slide my tongue in. God, if I knew kissing Ashley would be like this, I would have done it a long time ago. Our tongues twirl and mingle, and I soften the kiss, biting gently on her lower lip before pulling away. A question lingers in her eyes.

"As much as I want to, I can't take you on this dance floor."

Her eyes grow big as she quietly asks, "You want me?"

How could she think I don't? She's gorgeous, kind, and I love being around her. She could have any guy she wants, but for some unexplained reason, she's chosen me. Why is it so hard for her to believe she does this to me? Why is it so hard for her to believe how amazing she is? I shake my head in amazement. She needs to see and believe it. Hell, I'm the lucky one.

I grasp her hand in mine and place it on my chest, letting her feel my rapidly beating heart that still hasn't slowed. She looks at me with wonderment, "I do that?" She asks.

"You do more than that." I slide her hand down my chest, past the button of my jeans and onto the bulge at my pants. I lean my forehead against hers and whisper, "You not only make my heart race, but I want you so damn bad."

"Can we get out of here?" she asks in anticipation.

"Hell. Yes." It only takes those two words for her to grab my hand and walk us over to her friends. She let's go for an instant to walk over and whisper in Mac's ear. I see her nod and smile. She's immediately holding my hand again, leading us out of the club and into the parking lot. I guide us to my truck and open her door. Instead of getting in, she grabs me by my shirt and yanks me to her, looking me dead in the eye. "I need something to tide me over."

"So damn sexy," I say before attaching my mouth to hers. I start slowly this time. I want her to feel everything I'm feeling, and I put it all into this one kiss. I want her to know, before we take it any further, how much I care for her. I tease her tongue but don't dive in. No, this I take slow. I softly kiss her, adding very little pressure, and then use my tongue to trace her lips.

First her top lip, and then her bottom lip. She groans, "More."

I chuckle, but increase the pressure and finally give her what she craves. I slide my tongue in and tangle with hers. She tastes so damn good, and I want more, I need more. That's my mission tonight—to drive her to the brink and hear her scream my name. I get harder just thinking about it.

I back away and no words are needed. She slides into my truck and I get in, immediately grabbing for her hand. Her fingers intertwine in mine. The feeling of her hand in mine feels so right, and so good.

I drive straight to my place and the moment the door is shut, I pull her into my room. She begins to lift her shirt. "Stop."

She looks at me questioningly.

I begin to slowly advance towards her, "Let me. I'm going to be the one to undress you."

A worried look crosses her face, and before I can come any closer, she places a hand on my chest stopping me.

"There's something we should discuss first." She says taking a deep breath. "I know this is probably going to kill the mood, and I'm sorry, but I have to be honest if we're going to do this."

"We don't have to do this. I'll still be here tomorrow."

She purses her lips before saying, "You would, wouldn't you?"

I grab her hand; thread it through mine, place it to my lips, and kiss it softly. I watch her eyes widen. She gently pulls her hand from mine and begins, "I've always had these rules anytime I was with someone." She says and looks down wringing her hands together. "No one ever touched me in certain places and there was never any, you know..." She looks down, "I never allowed it."

I'm shocked, but thrilled at the same time. I slowly lift her chin so we're gazing into each other's eyes. "Why is that, Ashley?"

Her breathing picks up, "I never cared about any of them."

Her admission pleases me, but I have to know, "Do you care about me?"

Without hesitation, "Yes."

I already knew the answer; I can see it in her eyes. But hearing the word come out of those sweet lips is enough to send me over the edge.

"I want you to feel. I want you to feel all of me. Let me show you what it can be like with someone that cares about you."

She has no idea what this could do to me, and my heart.

Her eyes go wide like this admission is shocking.

She takes a deep breath and finally says, "Control is a hard thing for me to relinquish, and it's something I've always craved. For some reason with you, I don't feel that need. I think with you, I can let it go."

"I don't want you to feel uncomfortable, or do anything you don't want me to do."

"Please, touch me? I need you to touch me," she says, the second time with more force.

It's all I need to hear; reaching up and holding her face in the palm of my hands, I kiss her with everything I have. I pour everything into this one kiss and then make my way down her face to her neck. She moans and pulls me closer. I need closer, but I need her skin on me more. I back away, just long enough to pull her tank off and stare into her eyes. She smiles and reaches behind her, and unhooks her bra, letting it fall.

"You're so beautiful," I whisper to her.

She's perfect, in every possible way.

She smiles and yanks my tee shirt up and over my head and runs her hands down my chest. She leans her head and begins kissing my chest. My head falls back and all I can think of are her beautiful lips trailing their way down. It takes everything for me to rasp out, "No, we're doing this my way this time. This is about you, not me."

She looks up, standing up straight, and I see her eyes are filled with moisture.

"Ashley, I need to make sure that…"

She doesn't wait for me to finish and places a hand over my mouth.

"If I wasn't sure, I wouldn't do this…" She takes my hand and places it on her breast.

That's all I need to know. "Once we start, I can't stop."

"Then don't." she's challenging me. Okay, challenge accepted.

I bend over and pull one perfect nipple into my mouth, rolling it with my tongue and use my other hand to massage and pinch the other. She leans her head back and uses her hand to push my head further down.

"God, that feels so fucking good."

A growl escapes me. Hearing the word 'fucking' come off of her lips and knowing my mouth is the only one that's been on her perfect tits; I feel territorial.

She moves backwards until her legs hit the back of the bed and let's herself fall down, with me on top. I kiss my way back up to her mouth. My tongue sweeps her mouth and our tongues entwine. Her kisses are all consuming. I pinch her nipple one last time before sliding my hand down her flat stomach. I unbutton her jeans, slide my hand down the front of her panties and push them over to one side. The moment my finger reaches their destination she is hot and wet.

She moans as I whisper in her ear, "You're so wet."

She turns her head, looking into my eyes with heated desire, "Only for you."

I've never had a girl say something like this to me before, and it reminds me of how huge this is for her and for me. I begin to tease her clit lightly, rubbing my finger back and forth, before I slide a finger completely into her.

Suddenly, Ashley reaches down. For a moment I think she's going to pull my hand away, that maybe I crossed a boundary she wasn't ready to. She surprises me by pushing my hand deeper into herself. She sucks in a breath, "More…Faster."

So I do. I go deeper and faster, then pull out and add a second finger. She reaches down and starts rubbing my already hard cock.

"Girl, if you keep that up, I'm not going to last long."

She moans and begins pulling off her jeans. I reluctantly slide my finger, then my hand, out as she lifts her ass up and I pull her jeans completely off, followed by her panties, which turn out to be a thong. I take her all in while I stand, unbutton my jeans and yank them down with my underwear in tow. She lies there, with hooded eyes, and unabashedly checks me out. I can't help the slow grin that spreads across my face.

"Do I meet your satisfaction?" I tease.

She chuckles and it's the best sound in the world—so carefree and happy. "You more than meet my satisfaction. Come here."

I shake my head. "No. This is about you letting me do this. Not the other way around. I am going to make you feel so fucking good. This isn't just about sex to me. This is about you and me. Not a one night stand. Do you understand? "

I see a tear escape the corner of her eye and she quickly wipes it away. Gently I say, "You aren't just a piece of ass to me. God, you are so much more. Let me show you what you mean to me. Let me make you feel good. I don't just want *this* with you, I want so much more. I want all of you, Ash."

When the words are out, I realize how true they are. I want her in every capacity. I have concerns, and other people to think about. There are things she knows nothing about. But for now, we'll live for now and I will worry about that later. I come to the realization I more than like this girl. I'm falling for this girl, and I'm falling hard. I've truly never felt this way about a girl before.

She reaches up and cups my face with her palm and every worry and thought I just had washes away because I can see it. The same look is reflected in her eyes. She feels the same way I do.

CHAPTER 25

GONER

I see he cares, and I want him to see the same look reflected in my eyes. I've never wanted anyone like I want him. I lean up and he meets me half way, and I'm gone. Our mouths collide and his tongue sweeps in and tangles with mine. Gone is the control freak as I give myself to him, completely. In just this kiss I try to tell him everything I've been unable to say out loud. I'm not ready to say it out loud and make it more real. I'm too scared to. I've been left by someone who should never have left me, but she did. I'm scared of the same thing happening again. Saying it out loud solidifies it, and makes it all the more real and scary. I don't think I could handle Zeke leaving me. Tonight I'm setting all of my insecurities aside, and just be, with him.

His lips move down my face to my chest and lightly biting my nipples, which I never knew could feel so damn good, and then down to my stomach. My stomach has butterflies in it. I've never had anyone do this to me before. He kisses my inner thigh sending a tingling sensation throughout my body and it hums in anticipation. I watch him as his head lifts and he smiles wickedly, "I've wanted to do this ever since we first met." Then I feel it, a sweep of his tongue, sending my head back as my body arches up. He grabs on to my hips and holds me down while he devours me. His tongue glides up and down, flicking my clit. Then I feel a finger make its way into me and my body begins to shake. So close to the edge, closer than I've ever been.

"You taste so good." He pumps his finger harder, then adding a second as he leans back down, licking me furiously.

Before I know it, my entire body is singing and shaking from orgasm. "Oh my God!"

He slides his fingers out and gives me one last flick of his tongue before kissing his way back up me. He hovers over me, looking at with me with something in his eyes I can't quiet identify. Or maybe I can, and I'm just not willing to admit it to myself yet.

I attack his mouth forcefully, wanting to taste myself on him. Nothing I thought I'd ever want to do. It's erotic and I like it. I love tasting myself on his lips. "Hang on, sweetheart."

I know it's silly, and little, but I love the term of endearment; it makes my heart thump wildly. He reaches over to his nightstand and pulls out a condom. I can't help quirking an eyebrow up, which he notices and chuckles. "It's not what you think," he begins to explain. "I don't bring girls here, never have. But there's this girl. We're in a class together, and I've had the hots for her since I first laid eyes on her, and I really care about her. Like, I'm crazy about her." He gets serious, "I'm so crazy about her." He looks down for a moment before looking back up. "I just wanted to be prepared. Just in case."

"You're forgiven, now put it on."

He laughs and, without taking his eyes off me, glides the condom over his shaft. It's hot. Really hot!

I'm ready to climb on him because it's what I've always done. Instead he pushes me gently down on the bed and hovers above me. He uses a leg to push my legs apart and nestles himself between me. Looking into my eyes, like I'm the only girl that's ever existed, he slowly pushes himself inside.

Oh my Lord, it feels like heaven. He pushes again until he fills me completely and I wrap my legs around his waist, pulling him in even farther. We fit perfectly together. I wrap my arms around his neck and yank him down to me, capturing his lips in my teeth, biting lightly. "Faster," I whisper against his lips and he complies. Zeke leans his head down, twirls his tongue against my nipple and lightly bites it, sending me over the edge again. Two orgasms in one night is definitely a record for me.

Several moments later, Zeke follows and catches his weight on his arms so he doesn't fall on me. He kisses my lips tenderly before saying, "You are truly amazing, in every way."

It's with those words I know I'm gone to him. I'm in trouble: mind, body and heart.

CHAPTER 26

YOUR PAST DOES NOT DEFINE YOU

I wake with a grin plastered on my face and my body spooned against Zeke. His arm is nestled around me, tucked in and around my waist. It's as if he thought I would sneak out and he's keeping me from leaving. Yeah, that's so not happening. Last night was amazing. I woke several times in the middle of the night needing him again. I don't know how it was possible, but every time got better and better. It's like we were in sync and attuned to each other's bodies at that point. I never imagined it could be like this. I snuggle in closer and feel his arm tighten and then his hand splay on my stomach. My body begins to tingle, and I start to heat up from my very core.

"Where do you think you're going?" his voice sends a trail of shivers all the way down to my toes and causes goose bumps to pop up around my neck, making my nipples harden and beg to be touched.

"Nowhere. I wouldn't dream of it. I couldn't even if I wanted to, anyway. You've got me pinned."

He waits a beat before responding. "Hmm, I certainly didn't want you running away when you woke up."

He loosens his arms just enough so I can turn around in them. I lean up on my elbow, so I can look him in the eyes, so he'll know how serious I am. His eyes are so expressive and his eyebrows are creased when he's deep in thought. My fingers, having a mind of their own, come up and begin tracing his eyebrows, trying to work the crease out of them.

I decide to be honest and lay it all out there. I can't go into this without complete honesty, not if we're going into a real relationship, which is something I want more than ever. "I've never cared this way about anyone." I look down for a quick moment gathering some courage and glance back up. "I've never had anyone care enough about me to treat me like I was special. I've never felt it, and I didn't deserve it."

"I don't believe that for a second," he counters. His hand comes up and pushes my hair behind my ear, almost petting me. It's soothing and gives me just enough courage to continue.

"There are things you don't know about me. I wasn't always like I am now, or at least how I'm trying to be." He stays quiet, sensing that I need to get this all out.

"I was a real bitch. I tried to steal other girls' guys." I look down in shame. "I'm not proud of it, at all. I realize what a bad person I was, and I wanted to do better and start new when I came to college. God, I'm doing this all wrong! I need to start from the beginning."

I glance back at him and see the purest look grace his face. "There's nothing you can say that will make me not want you."

He's telling the truth, I see it in his eyes, which helps me gather all the courage I can physically muster. I begin where it all started. "My mom left when I was young. She wanted out, and my dad just let her go. She was gone, and in turn, I was left with a very cold man. I couldn't do anything good enough. I was actually a very good screw up." I chuckle harshly. "I made a lot of mistakes, and I never quit missing my mom. But she left me…"

I swallow the emotions down and continue. "Through high school, I was the quintessential 'mean girl'. I'm embarrassed to admit it, but it's true. I was mean and ugly. Like I said, I did everything to hurt others, and I would certainly take what wasn't mine." I sit up completely and grab onto the sheet, covering myself modestly, needing as much coverage as possible. I look anywhere, but directly at him. I can't bear to see a look of disgust cross his face. "I was warned, towards the end of my senior year, to stay away from a certain guy. Of course, I took it on as a challenge, but I should have listened." Zeke reaches over and places his hand on my knee urging me to continue, but also letting me know he's still with me. Taking a much needed deep breath I say, "I was assaulted by this guy in his car. I was lucky. The guy was caught before he could go too far." I feel his hand tighten on my knee. "This is where it gets truly fucked up," I laugh bitterly. "The girl that warned me? She was raped by him. She'd recognized him and warned me, but I didn't listen. It gets worse, too. I'd hit on her boyfriend and yet, she'd still warned me," I shake my head at the last part. I can't keep my tears from falling, and fall they do. Zeke reaches up and sits up on his knees, using his thumbs to wipe away my tears. I still can't look him directly in the eye. I'm scared; I know this. Scared of what he'll think of me. What if he sees I'm not worth his time? I don't know if I could bear it.

He cups my face in his large hands and quietly says, "Look at me."

I finally give in, feeling the courage to do so with his large hands wrapped around my face. "I'm not going to lie and tell you I don't want to crush the mother fucker that hurt you. I do, badly. God, I hope he's in jail." I nod my head in confirmation and see a look of relief cross his face. He gently rubs my cheek with the pad of his thumb, comforting me.

"We all have things we aren't proud of. Lord knows I do. It's how we learn to deal with them, and try to change for the better that defines us as a person. Your past does not define you, the here and now does. I wish you could see you the way I do. You are so much more than anything you've been through. You're trying to be better and in the end, isn't that what matters? I see a caring, beautiful woman that loves her roommate. I hear how you talk about Mac. You care about her a lot. I think she's probably the first genuine person to come along and care about you for you, and not what she gets out of your friendship."

He's right; he completely nailed it. I nod numbly, and wipe my tears away. How did I get so lucky? How is it this guy can see past all of my mistakes and can see me, the person I'm attempting to become?

I lean into him and lightly kiss his lips then pull back to gauge his reaction and let the sheet fall to my knees. He removes a hand from my face and wraps it around my naked waist. His bare arm wraps around me, pulling me tight against him, causing me to shiver. My breasts harden and my nipples pebble against his bare chest as I feel my breath quicken. His eyes darken and I lean up and kiss his neck, trailing light kisses down to the side of his mouth. His head tilts back, giving me free reign. I kiss down to his chin and then under his chin, making my way down to his chest. I lick his nipple and lightly bite it. Doing to him what he did to me, curious to see if he likes it. He must because I hear a guttural growl. I then kiss my way to the other side, doing the same thing, licking and twirling my tongue. He lets me do what I want and I take advantage of it. I feel this need to go into uncharted waters. Show him what he means to me. I push him back and I see a question in his eyes, not understanding my full intent. I straddle him and continue to make my way down, kissing him all the way down his happy trail. I run my hands down it and see his muscles ripple at my touch. It excites me and makes me want to please him all the more. I feel his hand land on the top of my head, lightly running his fingers through the strands of my hair. I finally reach my destination, excited and turned on to see him at full mast, ready for me. Placing my hands around his cock, I lightly lick the top and feel him buck. That reaction is all I need before putting my mouth around his cock and moving all the way down and back up again. I groan which vibrates against him, causing his cock to jerk in response.

I look up and see him watching me with hooded eyes and I can't turn my eyes away from him.

"I'm not going to last long, sweetheart."

I ignore him and continue to suck and twirl my tongue, using my hand up and down, up and down. I hear his breathing pick up and then feel him tug on my arm, signaling me to come back up. I reluctantly let go, but know this time I'm in control. I make my way back up and lean over him to yank a condom out of the drawer, which puts my breast directly in his face. He takes full advantage of it and latches on, lightly, making me groan at the contact. I never knew my breasts were so sensitive, having never let anyone mess with them before. Now I don't know if I could ever have them not messed with. I love the feeling it ignites in my body and makes my toes curl. He lets go and I move so the other one is in his face and he can do the same thing to that one. He chuckles and I feel the air of his chuckle across my nipple causing me to shiver, again. "You like that?"

"Oh God, yes."

"Good, I like your breasts and I like the reaction I get from you." I sit up; leaning back and tear the condom open with my teeth, watching as his eyes roam over me, taking in all of me. I take the condom and roll it all the way down his shaft.

"That is so hot," he says with a heated look.

I grab on to him, rising up, I position myself over him and slowly lower myself. He fills me completely and we begin to move in a comfortable rhythm. He holds onto my hips as I move up and down, with him hitting the right spot. He leans up and quickly turns us around so I'm on bottom and he's on top. I wrap my legs around his waist and tighten them, pushing him farther into me.

"Oh God, baby, right there; faster."

He kisses me senseless but moves in me faster and I come undone. I feel myself lean and then topple over the edge, never wanting to come back up. He quickly follows me, but continues to kiss me until his very last thrust.

"You know you've ruined me, right?"

I'm happy and pleased. "Good, because I'm not letting you go that quickly."

His face turns serious for just a moment; showing just a fraction of worry around his eyes. "I hope not." He says quietly.

He removes himself from inside me and rolls over, "I do need to tell you something, though."

I'm too happy in this moment to listen and jump up grabbing his hand. "First shower and then afterwards we can talk." He smiles and it melts my heart as he gets up with me, allowing me to pull him along.

We shower all right, washing each other thoroughly, but talking is definitely the last thing on my mind for the rest of the day.

Zeke

God, I couldn't get enough of her. After our shower, which ended up as another round of hot steamy sex, I finally talked her into getting dressed so I could take her to get something to eat. I certainly don't want this relationship to be all about sex—which, by the way, was fucking amazing—I want it to be more than that. Much more. We went from irritating each other, to lab partners, to friends, and finally to acknowledging there is so much more between us.

I held her hand everywhere, not wanting to let her go, and loving that she was with me. She seemed shy and a little shocked I wasn't going to let her go that easily. She's mine, and I wanted everyone to know. I'm a little Alpha in my own right. I always saw what kind of attention Ashley attracted, even in class. She's beautiful, for sure, but she is also so much more and, yeah, I want everyone to know she's taken. Basically, I want these bastards to back the fuck off.

I catch her looking at me when she thinks I'm not looking. It makes me want to yank her to me, right then and there, and go all cave man on her adorable ass.

Hearing her revelations did not deter my feelings for her, in fact it made me feel more. I didn't feel sorry for her; it made her brave in my eyes. All I saw was a gorgeous woman trying to do better, and who could ever fault her for that? I certainly didn't. I was shocked she'd been assaulted, and I wanted to kill the bastard. None of these things affected my feelings for her; they only grew.

I still need to talk to her and have the conversation that never happened. It's imperative with us going forward, and I'm scared as hell. Especially knowing what I know. Fuck, I'm terrified. I'm not sure what she can handle, but my life is what it is, and good or bad, I wouldn't change it for anything. But now I just have to find a way to include her, and pray to God she'll be accepting of it. I'm going home to my family this weekend. I miss them. I need to talk to them, as well, and see what they think. I need advice.

Taking Ashley at home was hard, especially since she knew we wouldn't be seeing each other the weekend. I kissed her long and hard, and poured everything I had and every feeling I have for her into that kiss. When I pulled away we were breathless and I'd leaned my forehead down to hers.

"I'll miss you while you're gone," she'd said quietly and kissed my lips lightly.

I'd groaned in frustration, not wanting to let her go, but knowing that I had to.

"I'll make it up to you when I get back. Deal?" I'd promised.

"I'm counting on it," she'd said with a twinkle in her eye.

A friend of hers that lives down the hall interrupted us and I'd almost pummeled him for the disruption. I'd let it go though, knowing he was a friend of hers.

She'd told her friend Austin to shut it while staring at me, but had laughed.

Ah, I knew that name. The douche from the club, I remember.

I reluctantly let her go after kissing her again. "I'll call you some time tomorrow."

She'd smiled and kissed me again quickly, opened her door and slid in, closing it behind her.

I'd made my way past the douche bag's door and saw him standing in the doorway.

"Don't hurt her," he'd growled.

"I don't plan on it." Secretly, I was scared I would do that very thing.

"She's my friend, and I watch out for my friends." He'd replied seriously.

I'd nodded in understanding.

He'd pushed off the wall and walked closer. "I shouldn't be saying this at all, but she's never given anyone else the time of day. Lord knows they've tried. You're the first, so don't screw it up." He growled the last part.

I nodded again and replied, "Thanks, I appreciate it." I held my hand out and he shook it. It's a guy thing. We now had a mutual understanding and respect.

Truthfully, it was nice to know someone cared enough about Ashley to go to such lengths to warn me, and it made me respect him more. She was lucky to have someone care enough to have her back. I'd gone back to my dorm room and packed my things then took off for home. I was elated and scared at the same time. Elated for what awaited me at home, and scared at what it could all mean when I got back to school. All I knew is that I was crazy about Ashley, more than crazy. I was falling head over heels for her, and I was terrified it all could come crashing down and topple me over.

CHAPTER 28

JUNK FOOD AND MOVIES

I walk into my apartment to find Mac sitting on the couch with a huge shit-eating grin on her face.

"What?" I ask, innocently. But I can't stop the grin that takes over my entire face.

She glances down at her watch. "That was some night." She says playfully.

I sit down on the couch, with no clue where to start. "It was perfect." It's all I've got.

"So I take it he likes you?" she laughs. "Oh girl, I'm going to need more than that."

So I start from the very beginning at the club and end at being dropped off. I let some tidbits stay between Zeke and me.

She cocks her head to the side, "You love him, don't you?"

I take a moment to collect my thoughts. "Yes, I think I do. It still amazes me that he wants me, ya know?"

"Nope, I sure don't know. You are one hell of a catch, and anyone would be lucky to have you. Zeke sure is a lucky guy. Something tells me he already knows that, too," she smiles.

"Thank you."

"For what? Ash, I only speak the truth, and it's about time you start to believe it. New beginnings remember? You're dad sure has done a number on you." She taps her lip with her finger, "Have you heard from him at all?"

Now that she mentions it, "I haven't, which is odd."

"Count your blessings, girlfriend, because that would have certainly been a mood killer."

I cringe at the thought. "Ugh, stop it. The thought makes me want to poke my eyeballs out with a pencil." She laughs, clearly finding herself very funny. "Okay, so enough about me. What did I miss? What about you?"

She evades my eyes and I can tell she doesn't want to talk about it, but I'm her friend and as much as she's been there for me, I will be there for her. "Spill."

"Well, Austin's bitch of a girlfriend showed up, and that wasn't fun. She really isn't a nice person, ya know? I know he cares about her and they have history, but dang, I couldn't deal with it." She visibly shudders. "We were all dancing, all of us just having a good time. She showed up and got jealous and they ended up in a screaming match and then he left. I hung out with Nick and Ian, and we danced. I mean, come on, we're all just friends. Ian left to answer his phone because his girlfriend was calling. So it was just Nick and me. Nick leaned in and kissed me. I like him a lot, but as a friend, nothing more; I'm not ready for anything else." She fidgets with her phone, twirling it around and around. Sighing she says, "I just don't want it to ruin our friendship. I'm scared that it has."

"Well, what did you do?"

"I pushed him away and told him I was sorry, but I didn't look at him like that."

I whistled, "Okay, so you knocked his ego down some, I'm sure he'll be fine. I mean come on, it' Nick after all."

Not looking at all that convinced she says, "Yeah, I'm sure your right. I mean, Ash, he's hot. Like really hot, but I just don't see him like that."

I wrap my arms around my friend, who's so concerned about hurting a friend's feelings, and it makes me love her more. She's a good person who has an extremely good heart. "Why don't we spend the rest of the weekend in, eating junk food and watching movies?"

"You're pretty good at this friend stuff, even if you don't see it yet." She says, nudging my shoulder.

I inwardly smile and say, "Best compliment ever!"

That's how I spend my weekend, eating junk food and watching movies in my pajamas. True to Zeke's word, he called me the next day. He seemed a bit off, but I shrugged it off knowing if he didn't want to talk to me, then he wouldn't have called.

I'm excited to see him on Monday in class. Who would've thought I'd be looking forward to class so much?

CHAPTER 29

HEEBIE-JEEBIES

I wake excited as hell. Zeke called me last night when he got home. He seemed sad to be gone from his family, but excited to talk to me. I wish I had the kind of relationship with my family that he does. I can't imagine not wanting to leave them. I can't fathom it.

I dress carefully. I'm not sure why, it's not as if Zeke's going to care what I'm wearing. I realize I'm nervous. It's the first time we'll be together since before he left. Since we christened his bedroom and his shower. I get all hot and bothered just thinking about him and us.

I hear a knock on the door, and Mac pokes her head in and smirks. "Quit day dreaming and get your ass in gear, or you're going to be late."

"How the hell do you do that?" I ask, laughing.

"Girl, it's written all over your face."

"Oh."

I grab my bag and see a cup of coffee I hope is for me.

"Don't forget your coffee."

Score!

"Thanks, I'll see you after classes. My history class was moved to this afternoon, right after chemistry, so it'll be late." I say as I fly out the door, waving my hand goodbye and rush to my English class.

I get to the door and see Nick sitting in the seat right next to mine waiting on me. I slow my descent, not wanting to gain any attention and plop down. I quickly glance up front, too, and notice Forrester has his eyes on me.

Damn.

I do my best to ignore it, but I can feel his gaze on me.

I chat with Nick, who seems okay after the kiss he shared with Mac. I was a little concerned it would be weird, but so far, so good.

Class begins and I get ready to take notes. I listen and begin writing everything down, careful not to miss a thing. We are then given independent study and instructed to read several chapters on our own. I still feel eyes on me, and I try hard not to glance up, but unfortunately my eyes betray me. I look up to see Forrester is full on staring at me, and not being careful about it, either. I see his lips tip down in a half smile/smirk that gives me the heebie-jeebies. I look away quickly, and glance around to see if it is obvious to anyone else. Sure enough, a quick glance to my right shows, not only has Nick noticed, but so did the same girl that's given me attitude in the past. My heart begins to race, and I look back down at my textbook, trying to pretend I'm reading. I can't concentrate and I just stare at empty words until class is over and we're dismissed. I quickly pack my things and try to escape with Nick, when I hear my name being called.

"Ms. Davis, a word please?"

I stop in my tracks, and the words fuck, fuck and shit echo through my head.

Nick gently touches my arm and says, "I'll wait for you as long as I can before my next class, but I can't be late. He'll skewer me for sure. Good luck." I see the sympathy in his eyes, and I'm grateful he doesn't seem to be holding me accountable for the attention I'm receiving. I nod my head in understanding and make my way to Forrester, who sits at the desk in front, looking smug.

"Yes, Professor Forrester?" My voice comes out shaky then controlled and I hate that. It makes me feel powerless.

"I'm looking for an assistant who would help me with certain tasks. It would mean some late nights, grading some papers and other menial things. Whatever I need you to do. There is a small salary, and it would look excellent on your transcript." Without missing a beat he lowers the boom. "I understand your father is a benefactor for the college."

My body wants to quake, and I attempt to tamp down my nerves. I can't let him see me weak and not in control.

Not a question, but a statement. The truth is I will desperately need the money, once I'm out from under my father's thumb, but Forrester freaks me out, and I'm sure I could find something else to help me financially when the time comes. I'm not about to get 'into bed' with this guy. I know this kind of men, too. They're master manipulators; I've seen them my whole life. My father is one of them. I'm sure Forrester will do everything in his power to ruin me for not getting his way, but that's just something I'll have to deal with.

Taking a calming breath I reply, "Thank you for the opportunity, but I don't think it will work with my schedule. I have three other classes and I wouldn't want them to interfere with the assistant job. I'm sure my father would agree. My classes should come first."

He looks surprised at my response. I have no doubt being turned down rarely, happens to him, if ever. I smile inwardly, liking the fact I've just burst his proverbial bubble.

"I have a class coming up, and I really need to go. Thanks for the offer, though." I don't wait for a response I just turn and walk as fast as I can out of there. I reach the door and spot Nick leaning against the wall waiting for me.

He waited for me.

I lean back using the wall to hold me up, and realize I'm shaking. I turn to Nick and manage a small smile, "Thanks for waiting."

"I decided I could handle being skewered." He says with a smile, but his face quickly turns serious, "What did he want? I know it couldn't have been good. The way he was fucking you with his eyes and all. God, can that guy be any more obvious?"

"He wanted me as his assistant, to do some menial tasks for him." I blow out.

"Are you shitting me?" He doesn't wait for me to respond but begins to spout, "Yeah, he wants you in his bed, and I'm sure I know what the other 'menial' tasks he wants done are. That mother fucker!" He uses his fingers and does the bunny ears.

Lord, is he riled up.

He stops walking and looks at me, "I'm sorry. It just pisses me off. What all did he say?"

I'm embarrassed to repeat it, but he knows a little about my dad already and knows of his so-called 'importance' on campus. Nick's become a good friend and seeing how pissed he is, and given what he's already witnessed, he needs to know. I tell him the conversation and reiterate that Forrester didn't say anything wrong, even if he does give me the heebies.

"The heebies?" Nick laughs.

I smile a little, "Yeah, you know, the heebie-jeebies and the creepy crawlies?"

"Girls come up with the goofiest things."

I have a several minutes before my next class and even though he's already late, Nick walks me. As we get closer, I spot Zeke already there, waiting for me. I notice his eyes widen when he sees Nick with me, so I try to assure him with my eyes that I have eyes for him, and him alone. As we reach Zeke, Nick reaches his arm out to him and says, "Good to see you, man."

Zeke shakes it and says, "Yeah, you, too," uncertainly.

Nick glances at me before heading off to his class where he's bound to get in trouble for being late. "Tell him, or I will."

"Tell me what?"

"Well, this wasn't how I wanted our first conversation to go."

"Ashley, tell me what?"

"My professor has a thing for me." I explain everything as quickly as possible wanting to end this conversation, pronto. I rush to say, "He hasn't done anything physically. He just stares at me."

"Can we talk to someone and tell them he's being inappropriate?"

"Zeke, he hasn't really done anything at all. He just gives me the heebies."

"If he does anything again then we have to talk to the administration, okay? You are my concern, and this guy sounds like a royal douche bag."

He takes my hand in his and pulls me forward. "I missed you." He leans in and gives me a sweet kiss on the mouth that warms me to my very core.

"Too bad we have class," I say mischievously.

"I know. Trust me, I know." He takes my hand, threading his fingers through mine and guides us into class. We spend the next hour and half taking notes and glancing at each other periodically, making googly eyes.

Zeke walks me to my next class and kisses me good-bye, promising to call me later. It's going to be a long ass day.

CHAPTER 30

UGLY GREEN MONSTER

Zeke

I loved going home to see my family, but I'd hated leaving Ashley, especially after the night we'd spent together. I had a sit down with my parents and discussed our situation with them. Their advice? Time would tell. Not very helpful in that moment, but I understood the jest and truthfully, as much as I hate it, it makes sense. They said to make sure she and I were on solid ground before bringing her in to that part of my life.

I couldn't wait to see her, and when I saw her walk up with Nick laughing, I actually wanted to punch the guy. I can honestly say I've never felt that way before. But then she smiled at me, and gave me this look that told me it was okay and that I was it for her. It instantly calmed me. I knew they were just friends. The way she looked at him was completely different than how she looked at me. When she looked at me, it was as if I were the only one in the room.

But then when Nick prodded her tell me about her Professor, I was ready to hit the damn roof. I've heard stories about a professor, but I didn't know what was truth and what was fabricated, or which professor it was.

During class I couldn't keep my eyes off of her, and only half-assed listened to the professor. All I could think about was getting Ashley alone. God, I've become such a horny bastard. Alone and naked. I had to tell myself to quit thinking about it, or I was going to end up with a massive case of blue balls.

I managed to escape the rest of class with only a little pain, and kissed Ashley good-bye, hating to part with her, but knowing we would speak later. It was going to be a long ass day.

CHAPTER 31

MY VERSION OF FAMILY

It's Thursday night, and Zeke, Nick, Ian, and Austin are all coming over to hang out and have dinner with us. It is the first time we'll all be together. I'm nervous because I want my friends to like him as much as I do. I know it sounds silly, but I've always wanted to have a place where I belonged. A large group of friends where we could all hang out and have fun; like a family, albeit a different form of one.

Mac plops down on the couch next me. "Penny for your thoughts. You've been quiet this afternoon, what's up."

I glance down, fidgeting, because that's what I do when I discuss topics that make me uncomfortable.

"Is it your dad?"

I shake my head no. "I haven't heard from him, yet, which is surprising, but no, not this time."

I lean my head against the couch. "Truth is, I've been thinking about my mom a lot lately. I've always missed her, but I've been missing her more and more. I think... I think since I met Zeke, who I care so much about, and not

173

having my mom to talk to about him is bothering me. I want so badly to have what others have."

My lips begin to tremble and can't stop the tear from falling. "I just miss her, you know? Why did she leave me? Why wasn't I good enough to stick around?" A couple more tears trickle down and I see Mac take a swipe at her eyes. "I just want to talk to my mom about everything that's happened to me and everything that is happening. I just want her to wrap her arms around me and tell me that it's all going to be fine. More than anything, I want to be told I'm good enough and I've always been good enough."

There, I've said it. I've said out loud what I've always thought.

Mac reaches her hand over and squeezes my arm, offering me a bit of comfort.

"I've gone so long on my own, not being able to confide in anyone. I've kept it all in here." I fist my hand and hit my chest near my heart. "I've hurt here for so long."

"I know I'm not your mom, but I am your friend. Everything you have been through, good or bad has made you into who you are today. You've taken what you say wasn't a good person and turned her into something extraordinary, and sometimes it takes horrible things to happen to us to teach us we need to change, to be better. I'm sorry you've been so alone, but you aren't alone anymore, nor will you ever be." Mac swipes her eyes again.

"I'm sorry I got so emotional on you. It's just been weighing heavily on my mind lately. My father will never give Zeke the time of day; he'd snub him first. Knowing dear old dad, he's got his idea of the perfect mate all picked out for me. Boy is he in for a rude awakening, huh?"

"First and foremost, Ash, you can always talk to me, about anything. Don't apologize. Ever."

I lean over, giving her a hug to show my gratitude, even though I've never been a hugger.

An hour later there's a knock on the front door. I'm in my happy place now, and excited to be spending the evening with Zeke and my friends. I open the door and see Nick and Zeke together. I quirk my eyebrow up in surprise and glance from one to the other. Zeke only grins his half grin and says, "What? We've bonded over our hatred of Forrester."

Well, that explains it.

I smile back, elated they're chatting away like old friends, even if it's only because of their mutual hatred for my professor.

Zeke sets the food on the table before grabbing me and pulling me to him. There's another knock on the door, but I don't acknowledge it. I'm too caught up in the set of dark chocolate-brown eyes that are so serious and staring intently at me.

"What?" I ask hoarsely.

Let's face it, if there wasn't anyone here, I'd be dragging his fine ass into my bedroom and doing a lot of naughty things to him, but I can't. Mac and Nick and whoever knocked on the door are here as well.

"You're just so damn beautiful." He takes a deep breath before continuing, "I can't believe you're mine."

The wave of emotions that pass through me is indescribable and I'm at a loss for words. In this moment there is no one in the room except him and me. A single tear tracks its way down my cheek without me knowing, and he swipes it away with his thumb. It's almost symbolic to me; like this man before me is capable of wiping every bit of hurt away and making me feel whole again.

His hand cups the side of my face as I lean into it, and reflexively, I rest my hand over his, holding it in place. He gently, but hungrily, swipes his lips across mine and I can't help the moan that escapes. He leans back, with a promise in his eyes this will be continued later.

"Are you hungry?"

"Shit," I breathe, coming back to reality and look around. I notice it's just the two of us. "Where did everyone go?"

The front door suddenly swings open and Nick hollers, "I'm hungry. Are you two done making disgusting googly eyes at each other so we can eat?"

I throw my head back and laugh, embarrassed, but also touched my friends were kind enough to see a moment between us and respect it. It's actually quite amazing, which is why I know it had to be Mac that dragged them out. I catch her eye and mouth a thank you.

She nods and smiles, doing a small curtsy, making me chuckle and shake my head.

I say my hello to the rest of the gang, and to Nick's delight, we eat.

The rest of the evening is filled with laughter, and lots of it. I've never had such a fun night in all of my life. Zeke fits right in and it makes my heart soar. As I glance around, watching everyone, I realize I'm not alone. These people are my family. Surrounded by these people, I will never be alone again.

CHAPTER 32

LINGERING DOUBT AND I LOVE YOUS

A month has gone by without incident, and oddly enough, no call from my father, either. Just several short texts, verifying I am, indeed, doing what I'm supposed to be doing, which I continuously roll my eyes about, are the extent of the contact from him. As if I wouldn't go to class. Please. I may want full reign over my decision-making and life, but I'm not stupid enough to jeopardize my classes. I've met with the campus counselor and filled out every available grant and scholarship application form I could possibly find. Turns out, because of the Warden pushing me so hard academically I'm eligible for several. Paperwork has been filled out, and now I wait. I've been assured it won't be a problem, and approval is really just a formality. Thankfully, I'll be on track and on my own to decide my fate for sophomore year.

Classes have gone well, and for the most part Forrester has left me alone. I still get looks my way, and he's certainly called on me in class enough times. I see the intent on his face. What he sees is a tall blonde who couldn't possibly know the answers, typical stereotype. I'm not to be underestimated, and I'm always paying attention. The look on his face when I've answered a question he thought for sure would trip me up is priceless. What he doesn't realize is this class comes easy to me. Now chemistry, that's a whole other enchilada.

Thankfully, I'm able to spend a lot of time studying with Zeke. Yes, we study. There's a lot less fooling around and loads more studying. He's serious when it comes to helping me. Again, my GPA is my ticket to freedom, and we both take it seriously, knowing I'm done with this class after this semester. That makes me sad, but excited. I will definitely miss having class with Zeke, but chemistry can suck it. Fortunately, my other three classes come a hell of a lot easier and don't pose a problem. I just have to finish this year.

Even with all the studying, I still have time for my friends. God, the word, *friends,* has such a nice ring to it. We've implemented Taco Tuesday and everyone comes over and hangs out. It's usually me and Mac, or me and Zeke in the kitchen preparing the tacos, with Nick being a dweeb and snatching up the grub before it's ready. I'm still curious why Mac hasn't given in to Nick, but I respect her wishes. If she's not ready, then she's not ready. If anyone knows that, I sure do. You can't push anyone to do something they aren't ready to do. I also can see how it could be detrimental to their friendship, and the hurt it could cause Nick. I know Mac certainly doesn't want that. I just want to see her happy. It could blow up to a big huge clusterfuck and we've grown accustomed to our group of friends.

Ian has also told us, as of next year Ryann will be transferring here, which we're all excited about. Mac and I are stoked; another woman to add to our group. We've spoken to her on the phone many times now, but she amazes me. She has so much trust in Ian; it bewilders me sometimes. She accepted us so easily, without meeting us in person, and never gives him issue with hanging out with us. It's funny, but a year ago I wouldn't have been excited about having another chick hang with us, or having any friends for that matter, but now it couldn't be any more different.

Zeke has spent the last two weekends out of town with his family and it's hard. I want so badly to spend it with him, but I understand his need to spend it with them. I just wish he would bring me along. I try to tamp the doubt that creeps into my head. Is he embarrassed of me? What is it? I've never been self-conscious before, but I've never felt the need to be either. I've never cared enough about a person to give two hoots about what they thought of me. Normally, the thought of meeting someone's parents would terrify me, but it doesn't; not his. He's told me a lot about them and his eyes smile when he mentions his mom. I can tell Zeke comes from a good family. His parents run a farm a couple of hours away, not too far from a horse farm I've visited before. Small world, huh?

Self-doubt begins to rear its ugly head, and I find myself doubting his feelings for me. I don't like this feeling at all. Mac sensed it and decided some retail therapy is in order, getting out and not being cooped up in the apartment. Sitting around too much only makes me miss him more. We spoke this morning, but it was short. A little while later I did receive a text message from him that got my blood pumping, especially down in the nether regions, but it's still not the same. One day soon I hope he'll invite me to go with him and meet his family. I heard a woman's voice in the background holler out the name Lara. *I didn't know he had a sister?* I put it in the memory bank to ask him about later.

Mac and I are headed to the mall on the outskirts of town, which I haven't ventured to since arriving at college. I've decided to take advantage of the warden's credit card before I'm cut off for good. A year ago, being cut off would have sent shivers down my spine and probably would have made me physically ill. I know, dramatic right?

Now, not so much. In fact, it's beginning to feel liberating, knowing it won't be too much longer until I have complete control of my own life. For now, I figure Warden can contribute to some of my growing independence. I want to re-do my bedroom in things I love that don't remind me of my father's house. This is a new me, and a fresh start.

I went into my room, sitting on the bed and began surveying my surroundings. Ever since I was a little girl, I've loved sunflowers. They've always been my favorite flower; you might even call me a bit obsessed with them. They remind me of my mother. I remember my mom buying a bunch of sunflowers for the kitchen every week. It always made it so inviting and cheerful. I used to consider anything that reminded me of my mother a bad memory, but not anymore. I've decided to incorporate something from my past and mix it into my present, so I'm decorating in green and yellow, which reminds me of a sunflower and a bit of my mother. It's bitter sweet. My personal change for the better has also meant I needed to come to grips with my mom leaving. Deep down, I know she loved me. I'd felt it in every smile, every book she read to me, and in every hug. Whatever the reason for her leaving me behind, I know she loved me then.

Zeke helped me remember one night, when we were curled up in bed, and he was holding me tight, wanting me to tell him about her.

"Tell me about your mom."

I was quiet for a moment before responding. "She was beautiful, patient and kind." I told him stories of when I was younger and explained why I was on the library floor the first time he'd seen me. His arms tightened around me, offering his comfort.

"Did you ever wonder why she left you behind?" he questioned carefully.

"Truthfully, I just thought she didn't love me enough to stay."

He hesitated for a brief second, seeming concerned, and replied, "Did you ever think maybe your dad wouldn't allow her to take you with her, or see you?"

I sucked in a breath, feeling the truth of the statement take hold, knowing the power my father possessed, and to be honest, I hadn't considered that. But now that it's been said out loud, it made perfect sense. How would that have looked to the outside world, losing your family? No, he wouldn't have let her take me. Because of his selfishness, I was left to endure a motherless childhood and for that, I never would be able to forgive him.

"Why didn't I ever think of that, or question him about it?" I'd asked, tears spilling down my cheeks.

Zeke rolled me onto my back and hovered above me, looking me in the eye. "Because sweetheart, you were just a little girl, and he was the only parent you had. You trusted him. Why wouldn't you?

I can't begin to describe the feelings that started to build towards my father at that moment. I felt a loathing take hold of me.

Zeke cradled my face in his hands, and whispered three words I haven't heard since before my mother left. "I love you, Ashley. I've been waiting for the perfect time to tell you, and I realized there is no perfect time. I love you, Ashley, with all my heart."

I couldn't have been more stunned. Hearing those words out loud was a feeling I will never forget. When you're not told often, you tend to get emotional and I did just that. I felt the truthfulness of his words and knew I'd been biding my time until I could tell him, as well.

"I love you, too," I whispered back.

His mouth crashed down on mine, and in between kisses were whispered, "I love yous."

We spent the rest of the night showing each other just how much those three, not so little, words meant to us.

Mac comes bouncing in, bringing me back to the present. "You about ready? I'm so excited to get away from this place. I feel like we've been stuck here for freaking months." She cocks her head to the side, "Oh yeah, because we kind of have."

I don't think I've ever seen her this excited.

I spend the day with my best friend shopping to our heart's content; all thoughts of any lingering doubts forgotten.

CHAPTER 33

I'M A PACKAGE DEAL

Zeke

I knew when I came home a decision would be made that was weighing heavily on my heart. I know I love Ashley with everything I am. However, I was still unclear as to how to proceed. I have no doubt she loves me, and I have no doubt she's 'it' for me. But how much can one person handle? She's been through a lot, and suffered so much. We've been together for almost a couple of months, now, which isn't long, but when you know, you know, and I can't keep this from her any longer, nor do I want to. It's not fair for her not to know I'm a package deal. This other part of my life is the most important thing in it, and my responsibility. If we're going to be together, I can't hide it from her any longer. I want her to be involved, and know all aspects of my life. I want to bring her home to meet my parents, have her love everyone I love, and them, love her back.

At the same time, this could be a deal breaker for her. She may decide it's too much for her to handle. I also don't want her to think I've been hiding this part of my life. I just had to make sure. I needed to know for me.

The thought of not having Ashley in my life is inconceivable. In a short period of time, she's become such an integral part of it. It makes my heart hurt thinking she might actually be gone, that I may end up losing her.

Sitting on the couch I glance down at the most precious little girl I've had the honor of raising. My daughter, Lara, is four years old and the reason I breathe. Every decision I make is made with Lara in mind. I'd put off college until now because I wanted to be home with her until she was older. It's not easy on my parents, but now that she's a little older, they seem to be doing just fine, with me coming home on the weekends. I miss her terribly when I'm away at school.

Lara snores softly, snuggled in to the crook of my arm just like she did as a baby. Some habits are hard to stop, and I wouldn't trade it for anything. My daughter is the air that I breathe, and as hard as it is to be a single dad, I wouldn't trade her for anything. As I watch her sleep, my phone buzzes on the table beside me, lightly shaking the glass and I quickly pick it up before it wakes Lara. I glance down and notice Ashley has sent me a couple of texts already. I smile, seeing she's been thinking of me, she misses me, and she loves me. I quickly text back, telling her how much I love her, and take another moment to think about how Ashley's going to handle the fact I didn't disclose I have a daughter.

I know as a parent, it is my job to protect her. I would never allow anyone to get close to her unless she was in it for the long haul. Her mother is gone and out of the picture. Has been since the day she was born.

I have no doubt Lara would get attached to Ashley, and vice versa.

Being a parent is something I take seriously, and I'm committed to it, but I can't ask that of someone else, especially someone who isn't her mother.

My mom walks in, "You know you spoil her." She nods her head at the sleeping beauty in my arms, but says it with a smile and obvious affection on her face.

"It's hard to put her down when I've been away all week long."

My mom sits down on the couch and asks me the question I've been evading. "Have you told Ashley about her yet? I assume you haven't."

"No," I sigh and look up, "I'm scared, Mom. I'm terrified she won't be able to handle that I have a daughter."

My mom cocks her head, examining me hard. "You love her, don't you?"

I don't hesitate, "Yes, I love her. Ashley crept up on me and was unexpected. I tried to stay away, especially because of Lara, but I couldn't."

"You know, I think everything happens for a reason. You've explained a little about Ashley's past, and I'm not saying it's going to be easy, but did you ever think maybe Ashley needs Lara as much as Lara needs her?" Before I can open my mouth to respond she continues, "I'm also not saying she's going to take this well to begin with…"

She throws her hand up to stop me from talking. I shake my head and can't help the smirk that comes up, remembering these talks when I was a kid. Basically you sit, shut up, and listen because you might actually learn something.

"I know your reasons and I respect them, and I also happen to agree with your decision in keeping Lara hidden. But, I want you to see it from Ashley's point of view; you've deceived her. Even though your intentions are honest and pure, she's probably not going to see it like at the beginning."

My mom's eyes begin to mist as she continues, "I also sense a change in you. You aren't the same man that left for college. I can see you love her, and I trust your judgment. I know you hardened your heart after what Kim did. This is the first time I've seen you truly happy." She signals down to the bundle on my lap. "I know you love Lara, but that's not the same kind of love. I want you to be happy and want you to be loved the way you should. I know this isn't a decision you've taken lightly. Ashley must be some special girl."

I didn't realize until now that I've been worried about screwing up. Hell, I did that four years ago, but then I wouldn't have Lara, and that I can't even fathom. As hard as it all was, I would never take it back.

I ask myself, "Is Ashley worth the risk?" The answer is, without a doubt, a resounding yes.

My mom begins to get up when I stop her. "Hey mom, thanks for watching Lara so I could go to college. If it wasn't for you and dad watching her every day, and forcing me to go, I'd never have met Ashley."

"I told you, everything happens for a reason, and you're welcome. It's our pleasure to watch our precious granddaughter." My mom signals to Lara, "She's pretty lucky, too, you know. She's got you for a dad."

Without another word she leaves the room.

It's funny, but hearing my mom tell me I'm a good dad, and that Lara's lucky to have me, is the best compliment I could ever receive. I lean down and kiss her on the head, when I hear the sweetest words ever to grace her mouth.

"Daddy, I love you."

CHAPTER 34

I SHOULD HAVE JUST SKIPPED

I'm running late to my English class, which has my fucking heart pounding. I over slept after staying up late on the phone with Zeke. He didn't get home until late, so by the time he called, I was already in bed. He sounded off, and when I woke up this morning I decided to have *the* conversation, once and for all. Every time he gets back he seems off. I've tried to let it go, but now it's bothering me to the point I'm questioning our relationship. I don't want to feel like this, I'd rather ask him straight out, even if it hurts. The insecure part of me thinks maybe he has a girlfriend back home, and he's two-timing her with me. While I try to brush off my feelings of insecurity, I need to make sure that everything is fine with us. I tell myself that infidelity seems very unlike Zeke, but really, it's only been a couple of months. How well can you really know a person in that length of time?

I rush as fast as I can to class and slow my descent as I reach the door. I question going in or just skipping. I decide that going in late is probably better than skipping altogether. I can't help the 'fuck' that comes out of my mouth and I take a deep breath before I walk in. I feel everyone turn and stare at me. I avoid eye contact and look straight ahead to my seat. I see Nick glancing worriedly at me then back to the front of the room.

Come on, I'm not the first to be late to one of his classes, surely. Damn, I wish I were invisible.

"Ms. Davis," Forrester sneers. "It seems you've lost track of time. See me after class."

I sit down quietly and don't utter a sound; I just nod my head in understanding.

Throughout class, Nick continues to glance between Forrester and me. I never glance at Nick. I don't need any more ammunition headed my way and now I question my decision to come through the damn door at all.

I should have just skipped.

As soon as class is over, I remain in my seat. Nick quickly whispers, "Good luck."

I feel frozen in my seat and I wait until every last person has left. I finally look at Forrester and he looks so smug, sitting there in his desk, like he's God almighty. I realize just being late has provided him ammunition against me.

"Explain to me why you were late."

Keep it short and sweet.

"I over slept."

"And why did you over sleep, Ms. Davis?"

Um, creepy much? How is this any of his business?

I look him straight in the eyes and give him the answer he so desperately seeks.

"I was on the phone late with my boyfriend, and I over slept."

Smiling smugly and basically ignoring me entirely he asks, "Have you given any consideration to the assistant's job?"

I catch him staring at my chest and giving me a mental mind fuck. I'm uncomfortable, and he doesn't hide his lust for me. I'm taken aback by it, not to mention entirely grossed out. He looks like a dog with drool running out of his mouth. It's sickening.

One second he's asking about why I'm late to his class, and the next he's wondering if I've thought about the job. What is this cat up to?

I straighten my back and basically grow a pair on the spot. I don't care if he's my professor. He's acted unprofessional, and I'm tired of letting him think it is okay. Instead of taking it, bowing down to him and just putting up with it, I tell him like I see it. There's no one here, so what do I have to lose? What can he possibly do to me? I'm acing his class and this is the first time I've been tardy. I've caught him in nearly every class staring me up and down, and I know for a fact it's been noticed by several other students.

Bring it on!

"No, I haven't. I don't have the time to devote to being your assistant." I say with bite. My hands begin to shake, so I put them in my lap and hold them with my legs. "Let's be honest, shall we?"

He looks at me with surprise, but also with intrigue and a slight smirk.

Sick fuck!

"You want me to be your assistant for more than academic reasons. Am I correct?" I don't wait for a response; I don't have to. I can see all over his face I've hit his intentions right on the money, and he doesn't seem to be bothered by it.

My voice raises an octave and I hope he can't sense the slight tremble in my voice. "See, here's the thing, I've got a boyfriend that I love, but that's neither here nor there. The key is I'm not the kind of person who would jump in the sack with her professor."

I used to be that kind of person, but no, not anymore.

He seems amused by my bravery, which kind of pisses me off. "I know your father, Ashley. I know rich girls like you, and you're all the same."

I don't think my heart could have beat any harder, and it resonates in my ears.

I take another stab at it; a different approach. "Look, you're a decent looking guy, and I have no doubt you can find someone your own age to have sex with, but I'm not interested."

He visibly bristles at 'decent', like it's a horrific word and degrades him. Interestingly, he never counters the fact I said he wanted to have sex with me.

"What will your daddy say when he sees you turned down a good opportunity? You think that will go over well with him?" He asks cunningly.

I feel a resolve begin to take over me, along with a strength that I never knew existed. Like a flash of light, I see Mac and Zeke urging me on, telling me I'll be fine and suddenly, I feel stronger. I pull my hands out from between my legs and begin to stand. I'm not weak and I sure as hell refuse to let him use blackmail with my father. Better yet, let him. I just don't have it in me to care anymore.

He finds me entertaining and when I stand his eyes once again roam up and down my body giving me the heebies everywhere his eyes land.

"You know what, Professor Forrester? You do what you feel is best; I don't care. Call my father, I don't care anymore." I gather my things, throwing them in my backpack and walk to the door. The moment my hands begin to turn the doorknob, he speaks, stopping me.

"This isn't over. You could change your mind. We would have a lot of fun together, I know you would enjoy it."

A disgusting feeling travels through my body, and I know he's staring at my ass. I turn the knob the rest of the way, but before I open it, I turn back to him. "No, I wouldn't. You do what you need to do. I'll go to the school and tell them you've propositioned me."

He laughs and shakes his head. "I doubt they'll believe you. All they have to do is see your record."

"My record? What are you talking about?"

"We are all aware of your 'horrific' experience at the end of your senior year."

Cold ice sweeps through me. "How do you know about that?"

He laughs a cold, calculating laugh. "Why your father, of course. He wanted to make sure we were aware of your situation prior to you attending. He also said you were very popular with the boys and to let him know if we saw a situation he needed to be aware of. Your own father didn't even believe you. Whose word do you think he's going to believe? Yours, or mine?"

I can't contain my trembling body. I feel betrayed in the worst way, and by my father, no less. I feel like I'm being assaulted all over again. But instead of wandering hands and biting, I'm being bitten and slapped on the inside.

I manage to yank the door open and say three words. "Do your best!"

How I manage that statement, I will never know, but I walk away then I run as soon as I'm no longer in view of him. I run like hell all the way back to my apartment. I don't even think about my next class, I just run.

CHAPTER 35

SHE'S MY FUTURE

Zeke

I know something is wrong when Ashley doesn't show up for class. I should have left, but I don't. I stay and barely listen, feeling guilty for not walking out when I had the chance.

My brain is racked with worry for her. I pull out my phone and text her. I don't receive a response, which makes me even more concerned. I find myself drumming my fingers on my desk, and receiving looks from fellow classmates.

I finally say, "Fuck it," throw my things together and I leave. I notice everyone's eyes on me, but I don't care. Something's wrong with Ashley, and I can't stay and wait for class to end. She means more to me than this damn class. She's my future, hopefully.

CHAPTER 36

GOING HOME

I cry, oh God, do I cry. I cry until I can't cry anymore. I lay there in the quiet; a messy puddle. I realize I can either face this head on, or I can wait for it to come and bite me in the ass. But really, that's just not an option for me anymore. With my mind made up, I immediately bounce up and grab a bag, just in case I need it. I rush into my bedroom, haphazardly throwing things in it. I grab my phone and text Mac, letting her know we'll talk later, that I'm going back home to deal with my father and I may not be back until tomorrow, and ask her to let Zeke know.

I should text Zeke, too, but I don't. He'd only want to come and he can't. This is something I need to do on my own.

I rush out of the apartment and lock the door. In my haste to get away quickly, I bump into Austin leaving his room. He's like lead and I bounce off of him.

"Slow down, little lady."

He notices my tear streaked face and quickly begins asking questions. "What happened? Did Zeke do this? I'll fucking kill him."

I shake my head and finally find my voice. "No, it's not. I've got to go." I stutter out, "I have to go home. I'll be back tomorrow."

Austin grabs my arm lightly. "Are you sure you're okay? You sure don't look it."

I try to placate him by joking, "Gee thanks, Austin, just what a girl wants to hear."

"You know what I mean, Ash."

"I'm fine, really. If you see Mac just tell her okay? I sent her a text already, but just in case, please?"

He runs his hand through his hair, conflicted. "Fine, but you better let me know you got there safely. Just call, or something, when you get to wherever you're going?"

I lean over and give him a quick peck on the cheek. "Thanks Austin, you're a good friend."

"I know, now be safe." He hugs me quickly, and I run out to my car and get in. I now have three hours to think about exactly what I'm going to say to the Warden.

This is it, I realize. I'm finally taking control, and I couldn't be more terrified to face him.

The three-hour drive didn't help me plan out what I'm going to say. If anything, my nerves went up several notches. It's now late in the afternoon, so I may as well drive straight to my father's house, knowing he should be home within a couple of hours. It's funny; I don't even picture this as my home anymore. If I think about it, I haven't really in years, not since mom left; it wasn't a home anymore, just a place to sleep.

I finally pull into the gated community and put my code in. I wind my way around until I reach the driveway. I pull in and stare up at the monstrosity I used to call a home. Hard to believe I really lived here. I was just here a few months ago, but now it feels like a lifetime. I grab my things, walk up to the front door and open it. My phone buzzes as I close the door behind me.

I trek up the stairs to my old room and slide the talk on my phone, an action I'm sure will lead to a pissed off Mac.

"Hey, Mac."

"What the hell, Ash? Why didn't you wait for me? I would have come with you! Zeke is going nuts!"

I begin the arduous task of explaining everything. When I'm done she's says, "Wow."

"I know."

"So you are going to have the conversation with your dad before Forrester can?"

"Basically. But you know we had to have a come to Jesus talk at some point. Something needs to give, and I can't keep going like this. I was hoping it could've waited a little while longer and be under different circumstances." After another moment I say, "You know it's not going to be pretty."

"I'm so sorry, Ash. I can't believe Forrester stooped so low. He's a creepazoid!"

"Trust me, I agree. The way he made me feel when he was ogling my body parts—ugh, it made me feel dirty." I shudder in remembrance. "So... What did Zeke say? Is he severely pissed?"

"Honestly, he hates the idea you went home on your own, with no back up. You know he would've gone with you, but I also know that would have made it worse. You need this to be one-on-one with your dad."

"So, he's not mad?"

Mac laughs, "No, I didn't say that. He's frustrated. He loves you and he spoke to Austin."

I groan, drop down on my old bed and lay down. "Shit, I'm sure that didn't go well."

"Ya think? No, he was pissed you spoke to Austin and didn't bother calling him."

"It wasn't on purpose. Austin just happened to bump into me when I was leaving."

Literally.

"I think he got a little jealous over that fact. Not the bumping part just you actually talked to Austin."

"I didn't do it to hurt him, I just knew he wouldn't take no for an answer. I love that he wants to protect me, but sometimes you have to do things on your own."

She's quiet for a moment before asking, "Have you thought about what you're going to say to your dad?"

"No, my head hurts just thinking about. I know what I'll say when I see him. I hope, anyway."

"Ash, I have no doubt when the time comes, you'll be able to tell him everything that's weighing heavily on your mind."

"Thanks for your faith in me. Because I'm doubting myself big time, right now."

"Are you going to call Zeke beforehand?"

I thought about it, I really did, but I can't. "No, it'll be a distraction I can't handle right now. He's already upset. I'll call afterwards. I don't know if I'll make it home tonight or tomorrow. I'll let you know."

We talk for a few more minutes before I sign off and lay down to nap prior to the Warden coming home. I know after he gets home and we have our talk, things will never be the same again.

Chapter 37

Zeke

Pissed doesn't even begin to describe how I'm feeling. Mac called me, but I'd already run into Austin on my way to Ashley's. Knowing he knew where she went, and I didn't, made me feel something I'd never felt before. Jealousy. I've felt hurt before, but the jealousy was a new feeling.

After speaking to Mac, who promised to let me know when she spoke to Ash, I went back to my place and just waited. When Mac finally called and told me she'd spoken to her and what had transpired with Forrester, I was even more pissed. The first thing I did, was punch the wall, which was pretty stupid. Not only did I hurt my hand, but I now have a hole to repair, too.

I sat on my bed debating what I could do about Forrester. I couldn't lose my scholarship. I had my daughter to think about, not to mention I don't want to disappoint my parents, so I did the only thing I knew I had the power to do. I called Nick.

Chapter 38

White knights riding in on horses are real

I wake up to a booming voice with no trace of kindness.

"Ashley, get down here now!"

I wipe the sleep out of my eyes, run my fingers through my hair, and make my way to my impending doom.

I walk down the staircase and go into his study, the place where he conducts business. Which is exactly what I am, business.

He doesn't lift his head when I walk in. He waits until I am firmly planted in the leather seat, right smack dab in front of his desk. He lifts his head for just a moment before continuing whatever he's doing.

"So, to what do I owe this visit? Especially when you have classes?" he demands.

I gather all the courage I can muster, continuing to remind myself I have everything taken care of. What can he do to me? Nothing. Absolutely nothing.

"I had a situation at school you need to be aware of."

Not looking at me he says, "What could possibly have happened that you had to come home? You didn't cause another issue with a boy did you?"

My heart races as my blood begins to boil. "What happened last May was not my fault, and neither was this. And it isn't a boy I'm dealing with this time." I bite.

He finally looks at me, giving me the attention I deserve by. It obviously took my tone of voice to get his attention. "Well then, what is it?"

I take a deep breath, for courage, as well to mask my embarrassment. "Professor Forrester has been propositioning me. He wants me to take his assistant's position."

Father laughs snidely, "That's not a bad idea."

"No father, it's actually a very bad idea. He wants me to have sex with him, and I refused."

I immediately feel the bark of his bite. "That's ludicrous! How could you make up such accusations? He's a respected professor."

I continuously shake my head.

"I'm not, I wouldn't do that!" I protest.

He's angry, and not even giving me the benefit of the doubt.

My hands are clenched tight into a fist. I feel tears begin to form, but I hold them back with all of my might.

"I told him I would not take the assistant position, and I would not have sex with him!" I remember my plan to get it all out and put it all on the table, feeling a bit braver.

You owe him nothing. This is about you, and you alone.

"I'm going to the school board about him propositioning me, with or without your blessing."

He's pissed and his face is turning a shade of red I haven't seen in quite some time. "Don't do anything, Ashley, that you can't take back. You do this, and you're done. I won't have you embarrassing me further."

I stand up, and doing so makes me feel less small and talked down to.

"I'm doing what is right. Cut me off, I don't care! I will pay for my own college, and take classes I want to take. I've already got scholarships and grants waiting for me. This is my life anyway, although you've never allowed me any level of control. Well, I'm taking my control back. I'm done doing whatever you say, never asking me what I want! It's never been about me."

He bellows out, "You do that. You see how hard it is to pay for everything on your own. I won't be here to bail you out!"

I'm too mad to respond, and now that I've started, I can't seem to stop. So I don't. "What about mom? Did you make her leave, too? Ever since she left, I've felt like she abandoned me. Why would you make a mother leave her child?"

I can see it in his face, I guessed correctly, Zeke guessed it right. She never left me willingly; he made her leave. I don't need his confirmation. I'm sickened; for so long, I thought she would willingly leave me. I finally let the tears fall. There's certainly no use in hiding them anymore.

All of a sudden he booms and I swear his voice shakes the walls, "Everything I did was for this family!"

That's a laugh.

"It was never for this *family,* as you like to call it. It was never a family. This was about your precious reputation; oh my God, what would people think if you had to share joint custody?" The last parts screams sarcasm and I just don't care.

"Last time, Ashley, you go to the school board, and you're cut off, done. This is your last chance."

My lip quivering, I whisper, "Then good-bye." I turn and begin walking out and he hollers, "Leave your car keys. Try getting back to school now."

I nod once, acknowledging I hear him as I absently walk back up to my room and grab my bag. He doesn't come after me, he stays put in his snug little office. I throw my bag over my shoulder yanking my car keys out of my purse, throwing them on the table. I never thought he'd let me keep the car anyway. It's all about appearances. I don't fit the ideal appearance anymore, I never really did. I walk outside and pull my cell phone out to call a cab. Just because he's left me without a car doesn't mean I'm helpless. I already have a checking account set up that he wasn't aware of. The one thing I've had in my own name since I turned eighteen. I'd slowly been transferring money into it every chance I got. I wasn't stupid. I was preparing. Did I know when it would happen? No. But I was going to still have something to my name. I wait a total of ten minutes outside before the cab pulls up. It isn't until the cab driver asks me if I'm okay that I realize I'm still crying. I nod and ask to be taken to the nearest hotel. Fifteen minutes later, I'm dropped off at a Holiday Inn. I walk in and quickly get a room. I lock the door and with phone in hand, lie down on the bed and call Zeke. He's not mad, just worried. I tell him I need a ride and where I am. He says he's coming.

My white knight riding on a horse is coming.

I fall asleep thinking dreams really do come true. I have my white knight and he's on his way to rescue me, and this time, everything is going to be okay.

CHAPTER 39

HOME

I wake and decide to shower, noting the time. It won't be long before Zeke shows up and I'm feeling not so fresh. I hop in the shower and my entire conversation with my father replays in my head. I'm not as heartbroken as I thought I would be. I feel an odd sense of relief—relief at being insanely honest, for once. You would think losing my only family member, even if he was the one to oust me, would feel heartbreaking, but it doesn't. Don't get me wrong, it's sad, but my life isn't over, and I have friends that are more like my family than my actual family ever was.

I let the water cascade down my body, letting all of the bad wash down the drain. I picture everything I've tried so hard to change, and everything bad that's happened. This is it. This is my new beginning. I have finally taken control. I feel at peace.

I'm wrapping the towel around me when there's a knock at the door. I peek through the peephole and see Zeke standing there, looking anxious. I wrap my towel a little tighter and open the door, hiding myself behind it. *A girl's got to hang on to a little bit of modesty for crying out loud.*

He rushes through the door, closing it behind him, and wraps me in his strong arms, making me feel safe and at home. He is my home.

"God, I was so worried about you." He pulls back, staring into my eyes. "Don't ever do that to me again. Please?"

"I needed to do this on my own, but I won't have to do this again. He's cut me off, like I knew he would, and it's okay. I'm fine. I said what I needed to say." I avoid eye contact as I ask, "So did Mac tell you about Forrester?"

He gently tips my head back and says, "Look at me."

I do and see only love shining back at me. "You have nothing to be embarrassed of, or ashamed of. You did nothing wrong."

"I know, but…"

He doesn't let me finish. "I've got to tell you something. Nick and I went to a couple of administrators and made formal complaints against Forrester. You will need to do it, as well, but Nick actually witnessed it happen, and I was witness to your complaints about him."

I'm shocked beyond words, but also scared. My first thought is what if they don't believe me. "What did they say when you told them?"

"Basically, they said they were taking this very seriously. Having Nick witness his perverseness on several different occasions certainly helps your situation. We'll get through this. I swear." I believe him. With him beside me, I can get through anything.

I lean forward and kiss him thoroughly. He breaks off the kiss entirely too soon and leans his forehead on to mine. "I have to talk to you about something else. Something completely different."

I'm hearing what he's saying, but I'm not. I just know right now, this second, I need him, and in me, preferably. I drop my towel. "Talk after, right now I need you."

I yank his shirt up and over his head, and make quick work of the button on his pants, pushing them all the way down never breaking eye contact. He senses my urgency and lets me take control. It's liberating, but different at the same time. Touch is involved; his. His touch makes me feel alive. I walk us backwards until we fall onto the bed. He holds his arms out to keep from falling and squishing me. I wrap my arms around his neck and yank his head to me, kissing him with all I have. My tongue enters his mouth and makes a thorough exploration. I suck on his tongue and then bite it gently. He groans into my mouth, my hands trailing down his muscles and down past that sexy trail of hair. I grip him firmly and feel him jerk in my hands. I pump a couple of times and then swirl my finger across his tip, running my hand back down, repeating the movement again.

"Sweetheart, you're killing me."

He kisses my neck and uses his fingers to roll and pinch my breast, making me even wetter. "God, I need you now." I push him and roll him over, straddling him. I lean over the floor and snatch his wallet out of his pants pocket, handing it to him. He grabs a condom out then hands it to me with a playful smile.

I play back. "What, you want me to put it on?"

His smile grows bigger. "You're so damn sexy when I watch you tear it open with your mouth. And when I watch you roll it over me, it nearly undoes me."

I do what I've done so many other times, but this is different. It's intimate and special. From now on, I'll only ever do it for him.

I roll the condom down him slowly, loving seeing the heat in his eyes increase. Knowing I do this to him—there's no greater power. I lean down, kiss the side of his face and whisper in his ear, "I want you on top. Ride me, baby."

In one swift move, he flips us so I'm on the bottom and he's entering me. I wrap my legs around his waist, locking my ankles. Almost immediately we build a steady rhythm. He begins sucking and twirling his tongue around my nipple. I throw my head back as he begins to thrust into me harder, switching to the other nipple; it feels so damn good.

"Faster." I breathe out. He complies and I feel my insides tighten around him as I begin to tremble. His breathing gets harsher and I know he's close. Two more thrusts and I'm gone. He latches onto my lips and kisses me, following right behind.

"God, I love you," he breathes out, several moments later.

"I love you, too." I smile up at him.

Slowly, he pulls out and walks into the bathroom to discard the condom. He brings back a warm wet washcloth and gently wipes me clean. Something that would've been way too intimate had it been anyone other than Zeke. With Zeke, it's thoughtful and loving. His eyes slowly trail up my body and heat and love pour out of them.

"You're so damn beautiful. How did I get so lucky?"

My eyes begin to water. "You loved me for me, and accepted all of me. You never judged me, you just took me as I am."

"You're damn near perfect." He says lovingly.

"No, I'm not. Far from it." I say shaking my head.

Zeke slides into bed, yanking the covers over us. We're lying face to face. He slowly rubs a finger up and down my cheek and back up to my ear. "No, you're damn near perfect. You're it for me, sweetheart."

A tear makes its way down my face. It isn't a sad tear this time, but a happy and content tear. He wipes it away and gently kisses my lips.

I fall asleep, wrapped in the arms of my white knight that came to rescue me. Just like in the books my mom used to read to me. I'm pretty sure I fell asleep with a smile across my lips.

Chapter 40

Good and Loved

Zeke

I think about the last twenty-four hours—the waiting and the phone call I finally received. I was so damn scared for Ashley. I know she's strong, I've never doubted that. It's her asinine father I worried about. How much more damage and pain was he willing to inflict on her? Apparently, a hell of a lot more. As a father, I can't fathom ever turning my child away, no matter how old they are. He has no clue how absolutely perfect and wonderful Ashley is, no damn clue.

I glance down at her sleeping form and hold her even tighter. She's one of the two best things to happen to me. I feel blessed, and so lucky to have her love. She's opened up to me and told me things I know she hasn't told anyone, except maybe Mac. Her trust is something that's precious and it's certainly something I'm afraid I'll lose once she learns my truth.

Deep down, I know today has to be the day I finally tell her about Lara. Bad timing, I know, but I can't keep this from her anymore. I'll tell her when we get back. For now, I'll bask in everything that is Ashley, and make damn sure she knows how much I fucking love her.

I lean over and kiss the tip of her nose then the side of her lips.

"You sure know how to wake a girl in the morning." She smiles and then cranes her neck to the side.

"Oh you want to be kissed, eh?" I tease. I drag my finger from her cheek and down her neck and watch as she visibly shivers under my touch.

"That's so hot!"

She looks at my quizzically, her eyebrows scrunching. "What's hot?"

"The way you visibly shiver when I touch you."

She purses her lips together. "You can see that, can you?"

"Hell yes, I can, and I fucking love it!"

I lean over and kiss her neck swirling my tongue so close to her ear, making her shiver again before licking my way down her throat. I want to lick every place on her gorgeous body and I want her to feel herself tremble, especially when my tongue is inside her. I want her to remember how she feels in this moment. I want to hear her moan and hear my name purr from her lips.

I relish every moan and every heavy breath that leaves her luscious lips. When she reaches down and grabs my hair, pushing me deeper inside her, I groan. I love what I do to her, that I push her over the edge, until her legs tremble and she can't hold them any longer, until my name is the last thing she screams.

That's when I lean back up, kiss her with all I am, and slide myself inside her, wanting to make her come all over again.

I realize this may be the very last time I get to be inside her. I plan to make her come and remember me, and make her feel every ounce of love I have for her. She may feel I deceived her by not telling her. But by God, she will know I love her and she won't ever question that.

I make love to her until I know she's been good and loved.

Chapter 41

Perfect for me

I hated to leave the confines of the hotel, where I felt safe and loved, but we had to get back. I had to deal with the whole Forrester shit, as well as knowing I was truly on my own with college, but I'm prepared. I will finally get to take the classes I want to take and be who I want to be. It's exhilarating knowing these choices are now mine to make.

As Zeke drives us back, our fingers intertwined, and what I'm sure is a goofy smile on my face, I glance constantly at him. It's hard to believe that after everything I've been through, I feel like I've won. I'm a winner this time, and this hot-as-sin guy, with the dark brown eyes, is mine and wants me, solely me. I can't help feeling like I'm riding a high I'll eventually come down from. I'm not aiming for perfect. If there's anything I've learned, there's no such thing. But he's perfect for me. He gets me in ways no one else ever has.

He catches me looking and smiles, "What are you thinking about?"

I lean my head back on the seat and state as honestly as I can, "You. I'm thinking about you." I'm not embarrassed, not with him, not any more. I feel safe to tell him anything.

Instead of a teasing remark, I get a serious look, which takes me aback a bit.

"What about me? He asks.

I trail my other hand up and down his hand and wrist not being able to resist touching him. He's safe, home.

I look down shyly, which I never, ever would have done before. With him I'm vulnerable, and he holds my heart.

He suddenly pulls over to the side of the road.

"Look at me, sweetheart."

I glance up and see such a tender look cross his face, and I feel my courage mount.

"I was just thinking you're 'it' for me. You are my home," I shrug, like it's no big deal, but he knows different. It's a huge deal, and these are words I've never said out loud, much less thought, about anyone.

He leans over, kissing me long and deep, and when he pulls back a sigh escapes me.

Leaning his forehead on me he says tenderly, "Don't you realize by now, Ashley Davis, that you're mine? I'm not letting you go, and never without a fight.

I pull back, just enough so he can see into my eyes, "Promise?"

"Without a doubt."

Chapter 42

Secrets suck

The first thing we do when we get back is go directly to the administration building to fill out my formal complaint. I sit down with a couple of the college-board members as well. Everything has to be neat and tidy. They have to have a verbal account, as well as a written one. This takes a couple of hours to finalize, but thankfully it's not as bad as I first thought it would be. They don't harass or condemn me. I'm treated respectfully, which doesn't mean I'm still not nervous. I'm asked if I would like to contact my parent's. I explain I only have one but that my father has already been notified. Once I explained I'd gone home and spoken to my father regarding the events, I was excused from school with no penalty. Fortunately, they'd also removed me from Forrester's class pending an investigation.

I was so relieved, knowing I wouldn't have to see him again. I felt they'd believed me, regarding my complaint. For the first time I felt vindicated; that people were on my side. Zeke wasn't allowed in the room as I made my statement, which was completely understandable. He was outside waiting for me, though, and that's all that mattered.

I left the room walking taller, with a lot more confidence. It goes to show not all people are ass hats, and they aren't all in the Warden's pockets.

The moment I step out of the room, Zeke stands up. He smiles and puts his hand out for me to take. He looks proud of me; a feeling I've never felt. We walk back to my apartment hand in hand, not saying a word. There's no need.

Once we're in and the door is closed, I grab his hand, pulling him behind me, thoughts of making Zeke feel good running through my brain. He stops me in mid pull.

"Ashley, stop please, we have to talk." He disentangles his hand from mine and stays rooted to his spot, confusing me and leaving me stunned.

Something is wrong; I can see it. It's written all over him.

"What is it?" I ask carefully.

He looks scared, as if whatever he says is going to ruin everything we have. He wouldn't look scared for no reason.

He takes the deepest breath I've ever seen him take and begins. "Please remember I love you."

I nod my head, thinking everything good that happened to me eventually had to go away. Nothing good ever stays long for me. Why should this be any different?

"You know how I go home every weekend?"

That's when I feel it. The bottom drops out below me and I'm falling. "Oh my God, you have a girlfriend at home. I knew you were too good to be true. I knew there was something you weren't telling me, but I ignored it and just let it go. How stupid of me, I'm such an idiot. I swore I would not get involved with someone who had a girlfriend, I would not be the other girl." My body begins to shake and then I glance back at him horrified.

He vehemently shakes his head, "No, no that's not it. I swear." His eyes are wide and fearful. He walks to me, gently placing his hands on my arms. "Ashley, I only love one girl, and that's you."

"I don't believe you!" I holler at him. "Why would you go away every weekend, if not for a girl?"

"I do go home for a girl, but it's not a girlfriend, Ashley. I go home to my daughter."

I shake my head, there's no way he has a daughter. That's not something you keep from someone, not somebody you love and want to be with.

"Yes, I have a daughter. Her name is Lara, and she's four years old."

I back away feeling hurt beyond measure. I test the words on my tongue, "You have a daughter?"

"Yes, I do. I go home every weekend to be with her. My parents take care of her during the week."

"You have daughter you never told me about?" My voice gets louder, feeling I wasn't trusted enough to tell his secret to. "I've told you everything about me. Do you know how hard that was for me?" Tears leak their way through and finally begin to fall. I wipe them away with my arm.

"Just let me explain," he pleads.

"Don't you think that's something you should have done already? Explained?"

My mind begins to wander and another thought comes to mind. "Are you ashamed of me? Is that it? I'm not good enough to meet your daughter, or your parents?" But then as my mind wanders, other things come to mind. "What about the mother, your ex-girlfriend?"

He quickly spits out, "She's gone and has never been in the picture where my daughter is concerned. As far as my parents go, or my daughter, no, never! I have no reason to be ashamed of you."

"What's her name?" I ask quietly.

"Lara, her name is Lara."

"It's a good name, a pretty name," I stutter out. Hearing her name makes it all the more real.

I sit down in defeat, and throw my head in my hands, rubbing my eyes and willing the tears to quit before finally looking back up at Zeke. "Please, just go. Today's been a long day, and I just can't deal with it. I... I think I'm most upset you didn't feel like you could trust me. You kept your daughter a secret all this time. "

His eyes are red and sad. "I didn't mean to hurt you, I never would; not on purpose." He looks away and I barely hear, "Never on purpose."

He walks to the door and opens it. Before he leaves he says, "I love you, Ashley Davis, and we aren't through, not by a long shot." The door quietly closes behind him.

I curl up on the couch in a fetal position, crying, feeling hurt and confused. I don't know how long I lay there, I just know when the sun goes down, I haven't moved. I'm in the same position when Mac finds me.

Being the best friend she is, she sits down beside me, asks if I'm okay, and gently rubs my back, telling me she's here when I'm ready to talk.

CHAPTER 43

UNFORESEEN FRIEND

Zeke

I do the one thing that's completely out of character for me. I'm responsible and have had to be for four years, but right here, right now, I have no one to worry about. Lara is tucked safe and sound at home with my parents, and the one person that could give a shit is pissed at me, rightly so, too.

I reach into my phone and call the last person I ever thought I would call. I leave a cryptic message when he doesn't answer. I hop in my truck and drive to the dive bar down from the college, and for once, decide to be irresponsible.

I take a seat at the bar, show my ID and tell the bartender to keep them coming. I'm a beer drinker, I don't do hard shit, but I begin my wallowing.

I'm not downing them too fast, just enough to start a buzz. For shits sake, I have no desire to leave anytime soon. I have no place to go, and don't want to get piss-ass drunk too quickly.

I don't know how much later it is before I feel a slap on my shoulder and a body take the seat beside me.

"For you to call me, you had to have done something utterly fucking stupid." Austin jokes.

I grunt. He has no clue.

"In fact, I would have assumed it would have been Nick you called. You two seemed to have hit it off," he laughs.

"Quit being a jackass, man."

He throws his arms up in mock surrender, "Okay, don't get your boxers in a bunch."

"Look," I say sighing, "I called you because I know you respect and value Ashley's friendship. I can tell that. You wouldn't have threatened me if you didn't."

"Yep, that's true. I do. She told me off the first time I hit on her." He says laughing and his shoulders shake in remembrance.

The man inside me grows jealous, wondering if she liked it or not. If he didn't have a girlfriend would it be different? Would she be with him? I get a grip on the jealousy that wants to come out. I don't have time for this shit. If she wanted him, I have no doubt she'd have been with him.

He begins to tell me how they met and I'm proud my Ashley. How she handled herself, and didn't let anyone walk all over her.

"She let my girl have it and forgave me, putting me in my place." He shrugs his shoulders as if it's nothing. "She and Mac are the only friends that are girls I've ever had. I care about them and won't let anyone hurt them. Look, I knew when I saw you, you were hooked and wouldn't hurt her intentionally, but just in case, I had to say it," he laughs.

"Dick." I spout out.

He laughs even harder, "Yes, yes I am."

I shake my head, not being able to help it, but like the guy. I finally ask the question I'm dying for an answer to. "Have you spoken to Ashley, or seen her tonight?"

"Nah, I was dealing with my own 'girl' issues." He doesn't pull any punches when he asks, "So, what'd you do?"

"I honestly can't say if I fucked up, or not. It's not your ordinary situation." I swig down my beer and turn in his direction. "Look, I have a delicate situation, and I was trying to be careful about it. I just didn't go about it the right way."

I spill my guts to Austin. His eyes grow wide when I mention my daughter. He seems fascinated I have a little girl, and asks me twenty questions. Some I'm able to answer, but some need to be explained to Ashley before anyone else. She deserves to hear it all first.

Austin seems completely flabbergasted when I'm finished. "Look, I don't know what to tell you, or even what I would have done. I don't have a kid, but…" He looks as if he going to continue, but then says, "Never mind," shaking his head. I let it go, not wanting to push it, but sense there's something he's not telling.

"Look, give her time, man. It's a lot to process."

Time is what I'm afraid of. I'll be here, I'm not going anywhere, but I'm afraid I'm too much for her. What if she decides she can't trust me and can't handle the fact I'm a dad?

Austin, still bewildered by the fact I have a daughter, asks me a couple more questions I feel okay to answer. Ashley deserves to hear the important things from me first, though. I yank my wallet out and throw a couple bills on the bar, but I also pull out a photo of Lara. I hand it over to him.

"Cute kid," he grunts out.

"Thanks."

I put the photo back. Austin smacks me on the shoulder, "Look, I'll drop you off at home and then pick you up tomorrow so you can get your truck.

I nod thanks.

When I open the car door he stops me, "Look, I've seen the two of you together. I'm sure y'all will be fine. Just remember she needs time. She'll be fine."

I hope he's right. I really do.

I'm hurt. I literally regurgitated the whole ugly mess back up to Mac. She was genuinely shocked, and I could tell she had more to say, but she stopped herself, probably realizing I was in no state of mind to listen. I haven't spoken to him, in fact I went even further as to go to my chemistry teacher and ask for a new partner. Unfortunately, she shot me down flat, stating it was way too late in the semester to change. We would just have to work our issues out and deal with the situation. So I did what any pissed off chick would do. I texted him and said, "You do your portion, and I'll do mine." I know I'm real mature right?

I have this ache deep inside me that's taken root I can't seem to get over. It gets worse every day; feeling like a piece of me is missing. I'm ashamed to say I thought about finding a hook up, but quickly smashed that one into the ground. I can't do that to myself. I'm different; I'm not that girl anymore. I don't want meaningless sex. I have no doubt Mac would've had my ass, too, and I would have hugged her for it later.

On top of my messed up life, I can claim a small amount of good. It seems another student was witness to Forrester's advances on me in class, and also went to the administrators. He's currently on leave pending an investigation. That makes me so damn happy. I wanted to hug this girl, but they aren't able to tell me who she is.

On another shining fucktastic note, I have not heard from the Warden. Not one damn peep. It's been almost a week and a half and nothing. If I stop and think about it, am I really that surprised? The answer is a resounding no.

Five minutes before I have to make myself walk into chemistry. I'm scared and nervous. My plan is to walk in and ignore him. That's the plan anyway. This will be the first time I've seen him, since I sent him away.

He wasn't in class last week. I was all prepared to ignore him, and was shocked when he never came in. I'd be lying if I said I wasn't curious or concerned, considering he takes class so seriously.

I had a feeling he wouldn't be missing class again. That wasn't Zeke.

I finally gather enough courage to walk my not so happy ass in. I try to walk directly to my seat; ignoring the fact the man I love is sitting right next to me. My eyes betray me, and I stare directly at him and notice a look of longing I'm sure matches my own. I pry my eyes away and sit down. Throughout the entire class I swear I can feel him. He's so close, yet so far away. I feel his body heat and I can smell his aftershave. I keep my eyes faced forward trying hard to pay attention.

When class is finally over, I begin to gather my things as quickly as I can. I'm stopped by a hand lightly placed on my arm.

"Please, Ashley, can we talk? Not here, but somewhere else?" I can't help the shiver that runs down my body whenever he says my name. I shrug off his hand, as much as I'd like it to stay there, as well as other places, I can't do this right now. I walk away, just like a coward. I hear him hurrying behind me.

"Please, Ashley."

I stop and turn, "You have two minutes." I follow him outside to a secluded place under a tree. Like a bitch I look at my watch and act as if I'm really timing him. "Okay, begin."

"Ashley, I love you, but you've got to understand my reasoning for holding the information back. Being a parent is not a drive by for me, it's for life. Whoever I bring into her life, I need it to be for the long haul. I can't expect anyone to take on that kind of responsibility. I needed to make sure you and I were solid first. You're still young, and I've had to grow up so much faster. I can't expect that of you, it's not fair."

I stand there, stunned at his admission, never having thought about it like this before. He's right. Can I take on this kind of responsibility? It's not a question of how much I love him. I love him with everything I am, but this isn't just about me anymore. There's a little girl that could be hurt if we didn't work out. That's always a possibility.

I look up at him and whisper, "I'm sorry. You're right. I love you so much, but I honestly don't know if I can be what you need me to be." I wipe the moisture from my face, "I haven't exactly had the best examples, and I'm sure I'd be a horrible example for your little girl."

Zeke comes closer and tilts my head, and I'm looking directly into his gorgeous brown eyes that captivate me like no other. "Sweetheart, you don't give yourself enough credit. You are kind and good, and you care about people." He sighs softly, "I'm not asking you to be a mom to my daughter. I'm letting you know there's another person involved who would be affected by our relationship."

I know what he's saying, but in my head, I'm questioning everything. What if I got attached, and something happened between Zeke and I that ruined our relationship? Would she think I deserted her, like I've felt my whole life? I could never do that to her. I know for a fact I'd get attached, she's a part of Zeke. An epiphany hits me like a ton of bricks as I also realize I'm eighteen, almost nineteen. My father may have made my mom stay away, but when I turned eighteen, she would have had every right to contact me. To my knowledge she never has. I can't put his little girl through that.

My mind made up, and tears streaming down my face, I back away. His hands fall away from my face and he looks confused.

"I'm sorry, I really am. I think I'll always love you. I'll always appreciate everything you've done for me." I whisper, "I just can't."

I run.

Chapter 45

Facing the past

I decided I was done crying. I had to move on, but I couldn't do that, not quite yet. I can't physically move on with certain parts of my life until I dealt with them, and I certainly never thought I'd be doing something like this. I'm sitting at my desk in my room chewing on my lip with Mac hanging over my shoulder.

"I can do it if you want me to." she says timidly. She knows how hard this is for me, but somehow even typing it in and pushing the damn button seems like something I should do.

"I'm going to do it." I continue biting my lip.

"You know if you keep that up, you won't have any lips left. You'll have eaten them all."

"Ew, gross, Mac." It does the trick though, and I pop my lip back out.

"Okay, I can do this." I take a deep breath and type in Jessica Davis.

I nervously wait for Google to do its thing. A zillion matches for Jessica Davis come up. "Shit, there's a lot."

"Put in her name and associate her with your dad's."

Why didn't I think of that?

"Let's see what comes out then?" Instantly, one obvious match is displayed. I hover the cursor over the link, willing my hand to click on it. I close my eyes and click it.

Mac leans in closer and we read it together. The ugly divorce comes up, as well as the fact my father would have full custody of me. As I scroll down I see another link to more information about a Jessica Davis.

I know this is the link that will take me to my mom. All I have to do is click on it. I turn sideways and look at Mac. "I don't know if I can do this."

"I guess it's a damn good thing I know you can. Ash, I've been telling you from the beginning, you don't give yourself enough credit. You've got this. You need to know, and this is something I think will help see yourself differently and allow you to heal."

"Why do you always have to be so smart?" I smirk out.

"Push it, Ash, know once and for all. Plus, you've got me here right beside you."

I turn back and click on it; the results display an address I quickly type into my phone, noticing she's only an hour away. Not too far for a quick trip.

I snatch my purse up and turn to Mac, "It's now, or never. While I am feeling courageous, let's do it."

Mac trails behind me and out the door we go. I'm quiet on the walk to her car and begin fidgeting. We climb in, and Mac puts some music on while pulling out of the parking space and asks, "Have you thought about what you're going to say?"

I ponder it for a moment before responding, "I guess, I want to know why she stayed away. I'm not naïve; I know the Warden's deep pockets played a part in it. I don't doubt he pushed her out of the picture and it hurts I went so long thinking she'd abandoned me. I'd like to know why, when I turned eighteen, she didn't seek me out." I pause before continuing, "I feel cheated. I feel messed up on the inside, unable to move on based on my past."

She keeps me talking the entire time, and before I know it, the car begins to slow and Mac turns to me. "I didn't pull up to the house yet. We are down the street from it."

I take stock of my surroundings; literally see the white picket fence kind of houses—cute cottage-like homes, with cute well-manicured front yards.

My heart begins beating fast. "Okay, which one is it?" I ask looking around. "Duh, it's in my phone."

"It's okay, I remember, it's that one, 202," she says pointing. It's cute and I can imagine her living there. But even more remarkable is the rows and rows of sunflowers. "This is it," I whisper in awe.

"Do you want me to pull up?" Mac quietly asks looking at me.

Unable to speak, I just nod.

She drives up and pulls into the driveway and I begin to tremble from the nerves.

"Do you want me to stay here?"

I glance across at Mac, "Yeah, thanks for the offer, but as hard as this is, it's something I have to do alone."

"I'm here when you need me," she smiles encouragingly.

I open the door and slide out, shutting the door behind me and slowly make my way to the front door. To be honest, my feet move by themselves. I truly don't remember travelling the distance to the front door. I don't even remember lifting my finger up to press the doorbell. I feel like I'm having an out of body experience.

But then the door opens, and an older version of me is standing there, looking just as shell shocked as I feel. I'm not sure how, but words tumble out of my mouth.

"Hi, Mom."

Her hand flies to her mouth, muffling a cry, as tears begin to fall. The next thing that happens floors me.

"Can I hug you, please?"

I can only nod. She tentatively walks to me and wraps her arms around me, while we cry together. So many years have passed, and yet, she still looks and smells like my mom. She pulls back and leads me inside.

What I thought might have been the end of the beginning is now the beginning of the end.

CHAPTER 46

REVELATIONS

Two hours later, Mac and I are on our way back home. I'm tear streaked, but beginning to feel a burst of hope. Hope for what lies before me, and for what could be. Hope for a future with my mom.

I turn to Mac, "Thank you so much for waiting for me."

"I told you I would be here for you, and I meant it."

"My mom explained some things to me, some I knew and some I didn't. I always knew my father was controlling, I guess I just never realized how much. He did so much," I say shaking my head in disgust. "When she said she wanted out and was taking me with her, he flipped a lid. He did everything to keep her away from me. He had money and she didn't. She didn't have anyone to help her."

I look at the window, watching the dark scenery go by. "She assumed he'd completely turned me against her, after all of these years of being stuck with him. I told her he didn't talk about her at all; period."

"Where do you stand now? I know you can't escape the past, but where do you go from here?" Mac asks.

"For now, we start back at the beginning and try to build a mother-daughter relationship; we go slow."

For so long, I thought I just wasn't wanted or worth being loved. Turns out I couldn't have been further from the truth. She never stopped.

I need to think. Everything I thought has changed, and I've been thrown for a loop. I need to reevaluate me, and try to learn to not be so hard on myself.

Zeke

Two weeks since I've held her, kissed her, or made love to her. I see her in class, but we don't speak. We aren't ugly, we just avoid. Every day, her face matches mine. There's a part of me that's been ripped out, and I don't know how to get it back.

The first weekend I went home, sat down with my parents and told them what happened. As much as I love her, I can't expect her to be okay with my life and put that responsibility on her; it's not fair. My dad patted me on the shoulder, not knowing exactly what to say and had left the room. My mom stayed with me and listened. With my mom there's no pretending. I was an emotional wreck, and my heart was breaking. She could tell the minute I'd walked in the house. Lara, having heard the door open had run into the room with a huge smile on her face and her arms opened wide begging to be picked up and hugged. I'd missed my Lara, and couldn't wait to see her. Hearing her call me daddy is always the topping on the cake.

I'd spent the rest of the weekend doing what dad's do with their little girls. My Lara, she's the best of both worlds: she's a girly girl, but also loves the outdoors. I play dolls and have tea parties, but we also ride horses together and play ball. There's nothing I love more than spending time with her. While playing tea party, I remember thinking how shocked Ashley would be to see me sitting at a little table, drinking pretend tea. I may have even let her dress me up just a bit.

My thoughts always gravitate back to Ashley. I've had the chance to date others, but no one has ever come close to grabbing me the way she did. I've even questioned what it was about her from the beginning that set her apart from anyone else. I always go back to the library. From the moment I saw her, sitting on that library floor with her eyes closed, tears streaming down her face, she had me. There was just something different, and vulnerable about her. Yes, she's beautiful, but there is just so much more to her, something hidden. She is the most real person I'd ever met. How could I not fall head over heels in love with her?

I knew it would never be easy, and I really didn't expect her to become an instant mom to my daughter. I just needed to make sure it was real and lasting. I know it could have been awesome, but I also respect her decision enough to know she still had her own things to work out.

As I finish my drive back to school I begin to question what happens when this semester is over, which is soon. Will I see her again? In passing, or in a class? I must be deranged, but I'd rather see her in class and have my heart trampled on, over and over, than not see her at all. Talk about a glutton for punishment.

I need to just let her go, but how do I do it? How do I let the most perfect person for me walk out of my life for good? And just like that, I know my answer; you don't. My mind made up, I head over to make my one last plea.

CHAPTER 48

ZOMBIE STATE OF MIND

I'm sad tonight and feeling a little lost. I'm not myself and I walk around like a zombie. I'm all cranky and Mac said I was beginning to answer like a zombie. I'm growling, that's what it is. I've resorted to growling like a zombie; even the bags under my eyes support my condition.

I've gone back and forth, back and forth, and even gone so far as to have out loud conversations, trying to convince myself I did the right thing. But did I really? Did I let him go too easily? Didn't he say he would fight for me? Am I just scared?

It's a resounding yes, to all of the above.

I walk into the living room where Mac, Ian, and Austin are all sitting around, watching television and begin to pace. Austin sees me walk in, "Did you decide to join the land of the living?"

"Har, har, smartass." I say continuing to walk back and forth, chewing on the lip that's on its way to being chewed completely off.

Austin stands up and walks over to me, stopping me in my tracks. "Ashley, do you love him?"

I nod my head emphatically.

"Does the fact he has a daughter change how you see him?"

I know the answer the moment the question is asked, and it all begins to make sense.

No, it makes me love him more.

I shake my head, "No, it makes me love him more," I whisper.

Austin, looking like his smug self, says, "Then there you go."

I glance at Mac and ask, "What do I do?"

Ashley throws me her keys, "Go get him. Tell him how you feel, and just be you."

I don't wait a second longer. I grab my purse and head out the door, like a girl who's got someone chasing her. I run down the hall and into the parking lot and hear a squeal from a truck pulling quickly into a parking space. I begin to walk to Mac's car when I hear my name being hollered.

I turn around and see Zeke at the truck. I stand there in disbelief. Hands shoved into his pockets, he begins walking to me. He looks good, so good. He has a piece of hair that's fallen over his eyes.

"Am I keeping you from somewhere?" He asks quietly when he reaches me.

I shake my head. He's disabled my ability to speak. I'm curious why he's here; more like terrified. My heart begins beating like mad, and it takes everything in me not to move in closer.

"I said I'd fight for you. Well, here I am. I'm fighting. I'm not asking you to be an instant mom to my daughter.

All I know is I love you with everything I am and you make me complete. I know I'm asking a lot. I know I told you this before, but you're it for me sweetheart and…"

I silence him with a finger to his lips.

He had me at sweetheart. Who am I kidding; he's always had me.

"My turn."

I drop my finger and take a deep breath, "I was asked a question tonight that made me think."

He furrows his brows together, and it takes a lot for me to not touch and smooth them out.

"I was asked if you having a daughter changed how I felt about you."

I see him frown, concern written all over his face.

"The answer is no. It makes me love you more." The concern begins to fall away.

"The fact you raised your daughter, and sacrificed for her makes me loves you more. I also realized the past doesn't define me. I want this life with you, and for however long. I want to be a part of every facet of your life."

Relief shines through, and his sexy-as-sin smile is back.

"I just have one request."

He grabs me, pinning me in his arms, exactly where I belong. "Anything."

With a sly smile I say, "You are going to take me to meet your daughter and parents next weekend."

He picks me up off the ground as his lips slam down on mine. I reciprocate and poor everything I have into our kiss. God, how I've missed his kisses.

Reluctantly, he pulls back and leans his forehead against mine. "I can't wait for you to meet Lara and my parents. I would love nothing more."

We spent that night making up for the lost time. As much time was spent making up, there was actually quite a bit of talking. I was dying to tell him about my mom and what had transpired between us, that we were taking our mother-daughter relationship slowly. My father was a lot more controlling than I ever imagined, and my mom was scared. Scared for me, and what he could do if she didn't stay away from me. She'd always hoped one day we'd be reunited again, and that he hadn't done too much damage trash talking her to me. The truth is, he'd never spoken about her and treated her as if she were dead.

Isn't it funny how things turn out? We'd both realized at the same time we couldn't be without each other; that this was home.

Epilogue

Thanksgiving

As promised, the following weekend Zeke did take me to meet his parents, Julie and Steve. They were gracious and wonderful, everything I thought they would be and more. The moment I set eyes on Lara, I fell in love. She's got Zeke's dark brown hair that falls in ringlets to her shoulders. She's got a heart shaped face with big expressive brown eyes, and the face of an angel. The moment I saw Lara with her daddy, I fell in love with Zeke all over again. I don't know how that was even possible, but I did.

Every weekend since, I accompany Zeke on his trips home. I can't wait to get there to see Lara. She's become a fixture in my life I can't imagine being without.

Now, here I sit on Thanksgiving Day, surrounded by family, feeling grateful. I look around, realizing how much I've learned over the past four months. One, you don't have to be blood to be family. I have my new family at school: Mac, Austin, Ian, and even Nick. Second, your past definitely does not define you, and sometimes, bad things happen to good people, but with good friends, you can get through it. I realized I had been using guys to control what happened to me, it was why I had the no touching rule, but in reality it was controlling me—until Zeke. With him, I learned to let go, and was able to let him in. In reality, the letting go to take a chance with him became the biggest step in moving forward. It enabled me to move on from my attack and to take back my control, without the need to be with random guys. Lastly, I learned how much I deserved to be loved, and you get back what you give.

I've decided to go a little easier on myself next semester and take classes I enjoy. I really like books and reading, and I'm sure a lot of that stems from my mom's love for books. I'm thinking of being a writer, or journalist. I'm not sure yet. The beauty is it's now my choice to decide. I also thought about getting back into dance. It's definitely something I love and I've missed.

About a month ago, Professor Forrester quietly resigned. I guess word got around campus that he was on probation. Seems the male population, along with a few girls, had noticed some rather crude and salacious acts by him and finally felt compelled to come forward. I don't think letting him resign was punishment enough. I just hope he doesn't do this to any other girls.

Glancing around, I spot my mom in the kitchen talking and laughing with Julie. They really seem to have hit it off. As promised, Mom and I are taking it one day at a time, but we've been able to begin to build a relationship. Mom never went into detail about the things my dad did when she left. That conversation was our first argument. I felt I deserved to know, but Mom had a different view. She strongly believes some things children don't need to know, particularly the ugliness that can happen between two parents, even if the child is grown. And once I'd thought about it, I really respected her for that. I've already seen my share of ugliness from the Warden and there is nothing to be gained from adding to that. He'd never believed me when it really mattered, even though I'd never given him a reason not to. I haven't heard from him since I cut the financial ties, and I'm okay with that. As I watch my mom, laughing with Julie, I smile and think how nice it is to have my mom back.

I'm curled into Zeke's side, on the couch, with his arm draped around me. Lara decided to snuggle up into my lap and she's fallen fast asleep. I absently stroke her hair and hold her just a little tighter. It's amazing how quickly she's attached herself to me, and I love it.

Zeke leans over, smiling and says, "You know, you're spoiling her."

"Oh hush, it's no different than what you do. Plus, we don't get to see her that often, so I'll take whatever I can, and spoil away."

Zeke lightly chuckles then says, "I love seeing how much you love her. She loves you a lot, you know."

I look up at him, amazed at the love I feel for both of them. "I know, and I wouldn't change a thing."

The End

Acknowledgements

First and foremost to my children: Gabe, Lucas and Jacob. I swear I'd be lost without you three. You three are the air I breathe. I still want to keep you through all of the fighting that ensues, even when I'm trying to write. I love that you all understand my love for writing and how important it is to me. I also love that you don't mind take out and when I do actually cook, you always make a point of telling me that I'm the best cooker ever in the world. Yes, for that, you will be kept. I love you so, so much!

Tami Norman, there's not really anything else I can say that I haven't already. You're my go to person; about everything! You are my biggest support system and cheerleader! You are a rock star. I swear everything you touch is amazing and you make my books so beautiful. Thank you for always sticking with me. I'd be truly lost without you. I love you dear friend.

Robin Harper of Wicked by Design, my friend first and cover designer second. Thank you for your beautiful work. You know me so well and you always know exactly what I'm looking for. You're stuck with me for life; I hope you know that. I love your face off!!

My stream team: Honey's you all rock my socks and I'm so grateful to you all. Marcia Woodell, Julie Deaton, Amanda Berisford, Caroline R Hattrich, Debbie Diprima, Emily Proffitt-Plice, Jena Eilers, Kathleen Williams Rider, Kristy Louise, Nanee McGee, Stefanie Kral, Tamara Debbaut, Tami Norman, Terri Cox & Sarah Goodman.

My editor, Rae Green, my pal first and foremost, and editor second. I love your guts, girl! I'm so glad we get to be on this journey together.

I would be nowhere without my fabulous and favorite bloggers. Into the Night Reviews, The Novel Seduction, Book Addict Mumma, Debbie the Book Vixen, Mommy's Late Night Book-Up, Up all Night Read all Day, Secretly Adorkable Readers, Evette Reads, Felecia Hickman-Amaya, Lara Feldstein with Mean Girls Luv Books,

Sarah Goodman, you're my twin, my other half. Thank you for talking me down from the ledge and just being there for me. You're always there when I need you. You are a fantastic friend and author and don't ever forget that.

Keep reading for a sneak peek of book #2 in the Changing Series

The Changing Series - Book #2

Coming spring 2014

PROLOGUE

JUNIOR YEAR 2011

I run as fast as I can, trying to meld away into the shadows with tears streaking down my face. I held it in as long as I could, but I'm human. The minute I turned they just wouldn't stay any in any longer. I can't let anyone see me cry, especially not the ones with the awful words that laughed and mocked me as I turned and sped away. How could he just stand there and allow it to happen? How could he pretend there was nothing there? How could he just let me walk away?

I knew I wasn't anyone special, but I thought he saw me, that he did see me. How wrong I turned out to be.

I wasn't popular, but we were friendly in class. When I spoke to him, he seemed to listen. The only reason we got to know one another was solely because he had a sister in gymnastics where I also trained. I'd been in gymnastics for what seems like my whole life. I lived and breathed it. I'm of Puerto Rican-American heritage and I have the body of a gymnast. Yes, my body is strong and reliable, but this also means I have overly muscular legs and defined arms and I'm flat-chested as hell. I don't have the body guys dream of but I'm certainly not ugly by any means.

But this? This I never saw coming. I thought when I'd received a note from him wanting me to attend a party that this was it. This was when he was going to ask me out on a date. I'd been so excited after school and taken special care to find clothes that helped make me look pretty. Clothes that made me look more feminine. I'd walked into that party with my head held high and immediately sought him out. Unfortunately, I'd also found him playing tonsil hockey with my arch nemesis, Holly.

Holly is the queen bitch in our school. She's the mean girl that you're scared of. She's the first one to ridicule you if you're wearing the wrong clothes, or if you're legs are too muscular, or your arms remind her of a guy's… or if you're me. I don't remember a day passing when she hasn't had an unkind word for me. If it's not me, she is bullying someone else.

Imagine the shock I felt as I approached the one guy I thought I'd made a connection with, thought was different, only to see his lips locked firmly on the one person that made it her mission to make my life hell. As if she was watching for me, Holly pulled back smirking as I approached. The next words out of her mouth were like a bucket of cold water dumped over my head.

"Did you really think he wrote that note?" She looks me up and down and then motions to Reece. "Look at him and then look at you. He's hot and you're just…not."

In that moment I vowed to never look at Reece Shaw, ever again. He didn't deserve any admiration from me. He certainly wasn't the boy I thought he was, the kind boy who seemed to like talking to me. What I was seeing tonight made me question everything I thought I knew about him.

I ran as quick as my legs could carry me, but it wasn't fast enough to escape the string of laughter that followed me, with Holly's raucous laughter the loudest of them all. As I turned the corner taking me well out of sight, I could still hear the laughter resounding in my ears. It followed me all the way home, staying with me until I cried myself to sleep.

Playlist for Changing Tunes

Music is a huge inspiration to me when I'm writing. Some songs I listened to more than others and for certain scenes. There are two songs that I listened to over and over again.

Waiting for Superman by Doughtry was the theme song through the entire book. It was inspiring and made me think of Ashley throughout and I really wanted to be able to get approval to put the lyrics of the song in its entirety in here but sadly that's a very hard thing to do. So this is my plug to Daughtry and for the record the entire album is fantastic.

The next song that would make me cry buckets and literally would help me write an emotional scene is *Breathe Again* by Sara Bareilles. I'm a huge fan of hers anyway, but the piano and her voice together are like magic. I would cry every single time.

Baptized by Daughtry
Cinderella by Daughtry
Battleships by Daughtry
Love Song Sara Bareilles
Gravity by Sara Bareilles
Chasing the Sun by Sara Bareilles
King of Anything by Sara Bareilles
I Choose You by Sara Bareilles
Uncharted by Sara Bareilles
Brave by Sara Bareilles
Hold My Herat by Sara Bareilles

Burn by Ellie Goulding

American Girl by Bonnie McKee

Slow Me Down by Sarah Evans

A Little But Stronger by Sarah Evans

Chillin It by Cole Swindell

Dust to Dust by The Civil Wars

Drive You Home by Parachute

Hurricane by Parachute

Overnight by Parachute

Didn't see it Coming by Parachute

The Other Side by Parachute

Waiting for that Call by Parachute

Disappear by Parachute

Whatever She's Got by David Nail

Clarity by Zedd/Foxes

People Like Us by Kelly Clarkson

Roar by Katy Perry

Mine Would be You by Blake Shelton

Red by Taylor Swift

Don't Let Me be Lonely by The Band Perry

I Will Love You Still by Darrius Rucker

Overcomer by Mandisa

Say Something by A Great Big World

What We Ain't Got by Jake Owen

Bruises by Train

Timber by Pitbull/Kesha

Drink A Beer by Luke Bryan

Ain't It Fun by Paramore

Stay the Night by Zedd and Hayley Williams

For the Love of a Daughter by Demi Lovato

Together by Demi Lovato/Jason Duruelo

Something I Need by OneRepublic

I Lived by OneRepublic
Human by Christina Perri
All of Me by John Legend
Runnin Outa Moonlight by Randy Houser
How Country Feels by Randy Houser
Goodnight Kiss by Randy Houser

A Note from the Author

Every assault survivor deals differently and we are in no position to judge. It's no secret that I am a rape survivor. I've been very honest and open about it. We don't all cope the same way. Some survivors regress, push others away and escape into a hole. They become quiet and complacent while others choose to react differently. They attempt to regain control back through sex. In my last book *Heartstrings* Tori dealt with her rape by falling into herself and keeping it a secret. While Ashley wasn't raped, she was attacked. Fortunately for her, her attacker was caught before the act itself could progress. She was fortunate but it still leaves a scar and it doesn't go away.

http://www.rainn.org/

or

1-800-656-HOPE

About the Author

Heather is a devoted mother of three gorgeous boys. She balances spending as much time with them as possible with writing, updating her Into the Night Reviews book blog and her day job. Her love of animals sees her home in Canton, GA bursting with numerous dogs and ferrets.

Heather campaigns passionately for anti-bullying initiatives and has a strong conviction to reduce peoples suffering at the hands of bullies.

A talented singer, who once dreamed of pursuing a career in that field, she has put that goal aside in exchange for her writing. A self proclaimed geek, whatever spare time she has is spent curled on the couch reading and listening to music.

Stalker Links

Facebook

https://www.facebook.com/Author.HeatherGunter

Blog

http://authorheathergunter.blogspot.com/

Amazon

http://www.amazon.com/Heather-Gunter/e/B00CMVYLR8/

ALSO BY HEATHER GUNTER

The Love Notes Series
Mature YA

Book 1 - Love Notes

Book 2 - Heartstrings

The Changing Series
New Adult Contemporary Romance

Book 1 - Changing Tunes

Book 2 - Gainers Grace-Coming Spring 2014

Book 3 - Breaking Ties-Coming Fall 2014

27350643R00150

Made in the USA
Charleston, SC
09 March 2014